Frankin Mouse

Christien Aurora Moonchild

Franklin
mouse
R.I.P.

Frankin mouse

My name is Frankin mouse I'm not like most monsters. I was created by an evil Doctor but I don't have any evil in my heart. So I was abandoned for not being evil and being a transgender monster, doesn't make things any easier. I might be a monster but I'm not a bad monster, my true to me name is "Anna Merry". I am a monster mouse who doesn't know what she wants in life. All I want is to find a place where I can fit in and be happy. I want to find more monsters like me. I would like a friend, so I don't feel so alone. Now I walk through the woods. Now I search for my happy ending, on my travels through the woods, I come cross another monster. They were sitting under a tree crying, when they saw me. Wiping away tears they asked me what brings you into the dark woods friend. I was abandoned by my creator for not being evil and being a Transgender monster. I hear you I was also abandoned by my own monster kin. My name is "Anna", what's your name? My name is "Jarred" it's nice to meet you "Jarred". Like wise to you as well "Anna". Hey "Jarred" maybe we can be friends? "Anna" I would love that and it beats being all alone as well. So "Anna" what do you want from life? I don't really know I just want to be safe, happy, and accepted for being myself. I wonder if we will come across anymore monsters on our travels. I hope we do maybe we could start our own colony. A safe place for monsters from all over so they can have a safe, warm place, with friends all around. That would be a great place to live. I think for now we should find some shelter in this cave for the night, and we can figure things out in the morning. Okay that works for me. For now we should get some rest. I can't believe this I go out hunting and come back to these thugs in my cave. Let's see how they like waking up to some monster in their face. Ah! Who, what are you and why are you in my face? My name? How about you give me your name first, and tell me why you are in my cave. I am "Jarred, 'and this is my friend Anna", we needed some shelter for the night. Now can you tell us your name? My name is "Lennzie, 'not Lizzy, or Lezbo" got it bird beak? Yeah I got it little ms fang tooth. So "Anna" why are you roaming around in the woods? I was abandoned for not being evil and being a Transgender monster. You? I was picked on by my sisters, for being a Lesbian, and I was banished by my tribe as well. I'm sorry to hear that "Lennzie". You can join our group if you want. Well it beats being alone, I guess I could join your group. I will also pick on you as well okay bird beak? That's fine with me little ms fang tooth. Oh and fair warning I have A.D.H.D okay so you're the hyper one got it. Okay "Jarred, 'Lennzie" I think it's time we head out. Yea okay sounds good to me. I can't travel in sunlight, so we need to stick to the shadows. I know of a way for us to get out of these woods. Sounds good how do we get out of the woods? I know of a mine that we can use. Sounds good how do we get to the mine? It's not far from here. Think you can fly there bird beak? Oh I think I can manage it ms fang tooth. That's good also I don't know if we can trust the carts that go through the mine. But we can give them a try. We are coming upon the mine soon. Wow "Lennzie" it looks like a great place for a monster to hide in. I have used this mine hundreds of times, and never have I seen any monsters in there before. Okay we should probably get going before the sun gets any higher. Yea good idea I don't want to turn to ash. Hey "Lennzie" what about this cart? Nah I want to take this one. Okay that works do you know where it goes? No but it looks like it goes somewhere cool though. Sounds good I'm curious on where it goes. Okay are we ready? Yep, pull that lever, and we will be on our way. Hey "Lennzie" this is fun. That's good to hear but I have some bad news part of the track is out. Bird beak get ready to grab your friend, and fly to the end of the tunnel. Okay "Anna", don't be afraid. We will be flying in 5.4.3.2.1. Now! Fly bird beak! "Lennzie" are you okay? I'm flying next to you does that answer your question? We should be close to the exit by now. Yes we are coming up on it. Looks like it dumped us off in a swamp. Yea that's not the tunnel I usually use sorry for almost getting us killed. It's okay. Good news is we are still alive. That's so true though I think we should try and find some rest and find some shelter for now. Sounds like a plan I need some sleep before night fall anyways. What about that cave over there? Yes that works what do you think Lennzie? She's almost at the cave, so I guess that answers that question. Let's catch up with her. Okay I think we should also get some rest for while "Lennzie" sleep for a bit. Yea sounds good we could use a break anyways. No! Ly'anna! No! I'm sorry! No! Don't kill her! Ly'anna! No! Why! Why does she have to die! Ly'anna I love you! I'm so sorry you have to die because of me! Lennzie! Lennzie wake up you were having a nightmare. No! "Jarred" 'it wasn't just a nightmare". "Ly'anna" was my lover, and she was killed by our own kin, all because we were in love with each other. Because of me she's dead, I'm the reason she's dead. "Lennzie" you can't blame yourself for her death. For it was the hatred of your kin that killed her not you. I think he's right about that. Huh? Who are you? My name is "Louis" I heard screaming and I came to see what the screaming was all about. I could join your group if that's okay? Yes you can join us. Okay mind if we camp here for the night? Yes we can do that. Hey "Lennzie" if you want to talk about "Ly'anna" you can. No! I don't want to talk about her! Nobody says her name got it! Yes we get it we just wanted to let you know we are here for you. What about you "Louis"? I am a were-cat I also don't have any real gender role. I think it's time for us to get some sleep. Let's get one thing straight fang nose I don't trust you as far as I can drop you! I think you should get out of here fang nose. Now that I think about it you were there, the day "Ly'anna" was killed by my father. No I wasn't. Yes you were you were sitting on a tree branch watching and laughing. I think it's time they go. Blood on a full moon they should go! They have been stalking me sense "Ly'anna's" death, they need to go before I. No! "Lennzie" I will handle this. 'You and "Anna" continue on the path ahead, and I will meet up with you when I can. Okay 'me and Anna" will head out after you and them are gone. Okay "Louis" come on let's go, and don't try to run, because I will catch you fly high and drop you and see how far you can crawl before I. "Jarred" not so hostile. We are off I will see you both as soon as I can. Okay "Anna" it's just us now. I can talk to you and only you about "Ly'anna". What was she like? She had flawless curly red hair, and just as perfect beauty to match, she had skin that would make angels cry. I miss her so much I miss her more than anything in this world. I'm so sorry about "Ly'anna". I can see how much she meant to you. There are no words to describe how much she means to me. If you have any more of your nightmares I'm here for you. Thank you "Anna" I appreciate that. You're welcome "Lennzie". Hey "Lennzie" I think it's time to head out now. Yea we should get moving. All we have to do is follow this path. That's what bird beak said. Hey "Lennzie". Yeah? Mind if I ask you about your sisters? Yea what do you want to know? What are their names? There's my sister "Rachel" she's got black hair there's not really much to say about that fang bitten fang bit. There's "Sali'zanna" she has blood red hair that's as perfect as her beauty. Then there's my crazy sister "Devili'anna" she has hair as black as her empty soul. But that's enough about them for now. Looks like we are going to have to go down through that trapdoor if we want to go any farther on our path. Oh man its dark down there yea its dark but it's a good thing I can see in the dark I will help you get through the tunnel at the end of this ladder. I hope we don't come across anymore monsters like "Louis". I hope so too. I couldn't stand "Louis" and I couldn't trust them as far as I could drop them. True maybe we can find enough monsters to start a colony of monsters like us. That would be nice I could use some more monsters like me. Yeah that would be nice. I wonder where this tunnel will come out to. Me too, I hope it's anywhere better than that stinking swamp. Yea it was kind of smelly there in that swamp, wasn't it? We are almost out of the tunnel; I can see a light at the end of the tunnel. Is it just me or do I hear water and the sound of birds? No...No I hear it to. Oh my this place is filled with such beauty. Yea it is I have never seen a place like this before in my life. There's so much color here. Is that? Is that a pair of rainbow phoenixes? I thought they were extinct. They seem happy without a care in the world. What brings you to the sacred forest of Althes? We were just following the path we found. Who are you and how are you talking to us? I am "Althes, 'this is my partner Solthes". We speak to you now through the power of the mind. Is this your forest? No strange one it is not our forest, we are the guardians of this forest. Is it okay if we find a quiet place to rest for the night? You may stay in that cave over there for the night strange one. Thank you. Why do you call me strange one? We can figure your friend out, but we can't seem to figure anything thing out about you that's why we call you strange one. Well "Anna" I think we should get some rest now. That makes sense now we know who "Anna" is we have heard rumors about you roaming around in the dark woods. We have also heard about your friend "Lennzie" here as well-being plagued by nightmares about her dead lover. Where did you get this information? Who told you about me mind speaker? That we can't speak of. Can't or won't bird beak. Both I guess you could say. "Lennzie" we need a place to sleep for the night. Fine... Fine I won't fight them for now. Goodnight "Lennzie", 'goodnight "Anna" see you in the morning. I think it's time we wake them. No not yet it's not time to wake them to that just yet. Why not "Althes"? Because it's not the time to wake them up to the truth just yet. Until it's time to wake them to the truth we should keep a very close eye on them. Fine…Fine we will do things your way for now. Quite they are starting to wake up. Good morning "Lennzie" "Anna" good morning to you as well. We trust you both slept well? I slept alright I guess. I didn't sleep at all and I don't plan to until you two tell us what's going on. I guess the worm is out of the birds nest now. I guess we have to tell them now. Tell us what worm breathe? "Lennzie" what are you doing? I heard them talking last night. Now tell us what's going on or I will turn you into a rainbow dress. Okay looks like we have no choice but to tell them now. Okay but just know we had no part in this. Oh just spit it out worm breath. Your worlds are at war with each other, there's also a group of monsters on the rise to fight against both sides, for rights in this world. So what are we supposed to do about it? You speak like we are supposed to be a part of this war you speak of. Are we supposed to be a part of this war? Ha blood on a full moon we are "Anna" doesn't even have what it takes to fight a war let alone help win one. We can train her how to fight. You can also get revenge for your lost lover "Ly'anna" as well. As much as I'd love to I made a promise with her that day that I would not fight to avenge her death. But I would fight to stay alive. We will see how things go. What's that supposed to mean bird beak? It means we will see if you kill or don't kill the ones responsible for "Ly'anna's" death. You say that like it's a test. Oh but it is, it is a test. Look here worm breathe I'll only kill to stay alive, so if I kill some monster it's going to be because they tried to kill me first. We will show you the world you left behind when the time is right. Well you might want to start training her than. We will be training you on your sword styles as well "Lennzie". How did you know I fight with a sword? That we can't say. It's not like you can travel through time or something. Perhaps she knows more than we think she does. Or she got a lucky guess. Who are we to say what she may or may not know about us? Perhaps, but we don't have time for that right now. Right.....Right I guess that's true we don't have much time. Alright "Anna" you will be training with me. "Lennzie" you will be training with "Solthes" on your sword style. Alright but we train at night. Alright "Anna" just follow my movements. Like this? Very good "Anna" you are a fast learner. Thank you I guess. If you keep this up you might end up training with "Lennzie" if this keeps up. Really? Yes but first you still have a few more things to learn about fighting, and you still have a few more fighting styles you need to learn first. Yea what is it? It's a sacred style called the dancing lotus. It sounds like a really cool style to learn. It's also one of the deadliest styles there is, and also one of the hardest to learn. I'm ready to learn it. Alright if you say so follow my movements. Hey this is kind of fun. "Althes" could she be the last one? The last what? I think she is the last legendary oracle. If she is what we think she is there's another style she needs to learn as well. Ah yes your right there is. Hey "Solthes" are you ready for my training? Huh Oh yes the first style we will cover is weeping lotus two sword fighting style. I've learned that already. Just follow my movements. Okay bird beak this is easy. Okay try this one dancing dragon twin style blade. Is there a style you will teach me that I haven't learned already? Okay here let's see if you have learned this one four dragons four blade dancing dragon style. That sounds like an epic style to learn. It's a legendary sword style never use this on some monster in training there won't be anything left of them. Use a lot of care when you use this move as well. I will I'll only use it in battle. That's very wise. Now that you have learned how to attack now let's see how your defenses are. Why should I work on that? Because you can't just go charging into battle. You still have defense training before you are done with your training. Why do I need to defend myself if I can kill the other guy before he lands a single blow on me? Wrong with that plan you will be lucky if you even see battle if you don't get yourself killed first. Well fine worm breathe if I do your training will I be able to see battle than? If you use your training wisely. What's that supposed to mean bird beak? It means as long as you use your training wisely in battle you will survive, you have learned a lot you should rest for now. "Althes" I think it's time for us to talk. Yes "Solthes" we should talk their training is almost over. Yes but don't you think it would also be a good idea to teach "Anna" how to defend herself? Yes I guess they should both work on defending themselves before their training is over. I think we should also have them spar each other a bit as well, so they can work on their defenses and strengthen any weaknesses and make improvements. Very well it would be a waste for all their training if they were to die in battle without any defense training. Yea it would be a waste if we were to just kick them out of the birds nest. Okay fine we will give them the training they need. Thank you for making a wise choice. I didn't do it for you I did it because I don't want to see all that training going to waste, and have it all stand for nothing. Well whatever your reasons are we should stop talking they will be waking up soon, true we will speak again soon. Good morning "Althes" "Solthes". Good morning "Anna" we hope you slept well? Yes I slept well thank you. You're welcome "Anna". Where's "Lennzie"? No! Ly'anna I'm sorry! Ly'anna! No! I'm sorry! I'm so sorry I did this to us! I'm sorry I got you killed! Please I'm so sorry Ly'anna! Ly'anna! Ly'anna! Ly'anna! No! Lennzie! Lennzie wake up. You're having one of your nightmares again. Noooooooooooo! Lennzie! It's me "Anna"! Oh I'm so sorry are you okay? Yea..."Lennzie" I'm fine. I'm sorry about your nightmares. Thanks "Anna" that means a lot to me. Anytime I'm just glad you're starting to feel a bit better. Yea I'm doing much better now. Okay you two now that you're both awake today you are going to be working on defending yourselves, from incoming attacks. Ha this should be easy. After we are done with your defense training you two will be doing some sparing. Sounds good to me bird beak. Okay let's get started. "Lennzie" you're with me, "Anna" you are with "Solthes" okay that works. Okay worm breathe are you ready? Okay "Anna" I'm going to strike at you and you are going to Block or Dodge to defend yourself from my blows. I Block like this? Yes very good "Anna" now I am going to strike at you twice this time, you will need to Block and Dodge. Okay I got it Block this one and then Dodge the next one. Very good "Anna". Okay "Lennzie" let's start your training with having you Block and Dodge four attacks. Okay this should be easy. Okay let's do this. Here we go ready? That's one this is two and Dodge on three. Okay this time I'll attack you six times. Alright I can handle that. I'll also mix it up on you as well. Alright one Block two Dodge three Blocks four Block five Dodge six Block. Very good "Lennzie". Thanks bird beak you're not too bad yourself. Okay "Anna" now I'm going to make it a little tricky for you, I will attack you six times and mix it up each time I strike. You will need to Block or Dodge. Okay I'm ready one Dodge two Dodge three Block four Dodge five Dodge six Blocks. Very good "Anna". Thank you "Althes" you are a good teacher. So bird beak when can "me 'and "Anna" spar? You can do some sparing right now if you two wanted to. Hey "Anna" are you up for some sparing? Yea I'm up for some sparing, I'm going to take you down as well to. Ha-Ha like blood on a full moon you'll take me down. Ha-Ha I see they have a lot of talk in them. They do, but they also seem to have a bit of a bond going on as well. That's good they will need any bond they can get where they are going. True they will need that and each other. Ha-Ha try and get me. Slow down and I'll get you "Anna". Ha-Ha I Dodged you. Nuh-Huh-No you didn't. Ooof "lennzie" you're not supposed to jump on me. Why not you make a great landing pad. Boy those two love to play around, don't they? Let them have fun their training is over tomorrow. Yea I guess you're right. You remember when we were young right? Yea I guess you're right they earned it. For tomorrow their new journey begins. Ha-Ha hey

"Lennzie" where'd you go? Up here short stuff. Oh man I wish I could fly that looks like so much fun. It is I will have to fly with you sometime. Yes I would love that.

To be continued...

Frankin mouse 2 Shattered Souls

Hey "Lennzie" we should probably get some rest. Yeah I guess we should get some sleep goodnight "Althes" "Solthes". Goodnight to you as well "Anna" sleep well. Goodnight bird beaks. Goodnight "Lennzie" sleep well. I hope they sleep well because they have a long journey ahead of them. I'm hoping their training will be enough to face the challenges that lay ahead of them. Quite we aren't supposed to speak of that. Yes but I hope so as well "Solthes". Just because we can't speak it doesn't mean we can't follow them and check up on them from time to time. True we could, but we also need to make sure they don't see us. True yes that is right as they shouldn't see us again until the time is right, but I think that's enough talk for now they will be waking up soon. Good morning "Althes" "solthes". Good morning to you "Anna" and you as well "Lennzie". Morning to you as well bird beak, so what are we doing today? Your training is over. So where are we going from here? Follow us through this portal. Oh my this place is amazing where are we? Welcome to the city of wavelet. Hey "Anna" look over there that church has a statue of my goddess Nixis. That's amazing "Lennzie" she is so beautiful. I know right she is the goddess of night, and she watches over us as a protector, and she guides us on our journey, and she holds us when we feel lost or broken. I'm glad you like her "Anna" I'm sure she's watching over you as well. But I'm not of the night or a vampire. Nixis doesn't just watch over vampires she watches over us all, and is there for us when we need her. Hey if you two are done soaking in the sites the city is under attack, and if I may remind you without weapons to fight with. Oh calm down bird beak, if you would have brought weapons with us we wouldn't be having this conversation, now would we? Fair enough we also didn't expect the city to be attacked either. There's a sword shop not far from here I'll go. "Lennzie" you will need to find a way to get to the sword shop, but with fights all over the city it might be tricky for you to get there. Oh hush bird beak you're not the only one with secrets. "Lennzie"? "Lennzie" where'd you go? I'm invisible hello. I'm going to the sword shop I'll be back in a flash. "Lennzie"? "Lennzie"? Oh great she's gone. Hey bird beak I'm back I also found this among the swords as well, and this one is mine so bug off got it. That craft work that sword is made from a great wolf's fang, with blood stones and emeralds going down the blade. I think we can defend ourselves now, we couldn't have done it at a better time to we are under attack. Well looking here alone vampire and her little friend throw down your swords, and we will give you a quick death. I don't think so slug brain. Have it your way then now die vampire! Ha I don't thinking so slug brain! Clang! Clang! Swish. Ah! How? How could I lose to a weak little vampire! I'm a vampire but I'm not little! You hear me I'm not little! I'm also not weak. Who else wants to taste the sting of my blade? Let's get out of here. Well looks like we are safe again for now, we should find a place to rest for a bit. "Lennzie" how do we plan to do that when the city is in chaos. I know I also know we need to watch each other's backs from here on in. Speaking of watching each other's backs where did "Althes" and "Solthes" go?

I don't know they just kind of poofed when the fighting started. We need to watch out for each other if we are going to survive, you're also going to need to start fighting monsters as well "Anna " if you don't chances are you won't last very long and our training would have been a waste. But "Lennzie" I don't want to hurt any monster. "Anna" here monsters are trying to hurt us whether you want to hurt them or not they are going to try and kill you. Do you want to die? No but I can't hurt others either. "Anna" it's not hurting them if you are doing what you need to, to survive if you don't start hurting monsters to stay alive you won't last long out here and I won't last long if I have to try and protect us both and fight these bad guys at the same time. We can find some safety in that clock tower over there for the night now let's get there and rest. From the clock tower we can take a peak of the city from there and see what our next move should be now let's get going. "Anna" you might want to learn how to stand up for yourself. I don't like hurting others "Lennzie" I can't hurt others. Standing up for yourself isn't just about hurting others "Anna" it's also not letting people walk all over you, I won't be around to help you forever you know. What do you mean? I mean if I have to try and protect both of us I'm going to get killed trying to protect you, you need to start fighting otherwise your training was just a waste of time. You will learn to fight even if I have to make you fight me. I don't know how to hurt any monster, well we are safe for now so you are going to fight me. "Lennzie" I won't fight you. Oh stop being such a fledgling "Anna" you need to fight as well. I won't fight you "Lennzie" I'm not going to fight you. You don't have any choice defend yourself you big baby. I'm not a baby! Prove it "Anna" prove you're not a baby. Fine! Now that's what I want to hear. Swish, Swish, Clang, Clang, Dodge, Dodge, Clang, Clang, Ah "Lennzie" get off me. Why? You make a great landing pad, Oh "Anna" if it helps imagine your enemies calling you a baby. Yeah I can do that but for now let's get a little rest for the night. Yeah that sounds good, goodnight "Lennzie". Goodnight "Anna" sleep well.

Do you think they will survive in here "Solthes"? I think they might have a chance now that "Anna's" started standing up for herself. But we aren't supposed to let them see us because we shouldn't be here. I know as long as we stick to the shadows we should be fine. We should get going they will be waking up soon. Where are we going to again? Shush we aren't allowed to speak of that it's not time to release that knowledge yet. Ah so that's where we are going. Yes and we should get going before they wake up. True I'm right behind you and we're off. Good morning "Lennzie". Good morning "Anna" how did you sleep? I slept well you? I slept alright, "Lennzie" where should we go from here? There is an old cathedral over on the other side of town we should check it out before heading out of the city. Okay sounds good let's head out. It's a cloudy day, so we should be able to travel faster, I think there's also a bread shop near the graveyard over there if we go west through the city we should be able to pass by it on our way out of the city, and get you something to eat "Anna". That sounds great, I am a little hungry. We can fly there if you wanted. Yeah that sounds fun it also sounds like the fighting has also stopped around town as well. We should get going "Anna" flying can be a little scary at first but it's really a lot of fun are you ready? Yes I'm ready. I'm going to turn into my bat form and pick you up if you are afraid of heights I'd say close your eyes or just don't look down. Ah wow "Lennzie" this is awesome and amazing we can get a better view of the city from here and looks like there's the reason the fighting in the city stopped looks like vampires. Yeah I see them as well we should probably get to the bread shop and grab you a quick bite to go we should be getting close to it now. Yeah we're close to it. "Anna" I'm going to start lowering us closer to the ground. Okay "Lennzie" sounds good I'll be in and out of the shop in a flash. That's good we should probably get to the cathedral as fast we can, with as close as we are now we should be able to run there from here. Okay I'll be in and out in a flash. Ok sounds good grab what you can but not too much just enough to eat for a bit. Ok "Lennzie" I'll be out in a flash. Hey "Lennzie" look what I found while I was in the bread shop I found a back sack. I also grabbed some cornbread, sour dough bread and it's really good you want some? No I'm good thanks we should get going we need to cut through the cemetery and head up to the cathedral from here, but we need to get going before they get any closer. "Lennzie" what's up vampires and not the friendly kind of vampires either, keep going, I'll catch up with you in a minute I need to make a quick stop in the graveyard for a second I'll be right behind you? Okay I'll keep going then, see you in a second. Okay I'll see you in the cathedral soon I got something to do real quick. "Anna" quick! Close the door behind me. They are close. We need to find a spot to hide for the moment. "Lennzie" what did you do back there in the graveyard? I had something I had to do real quick no big deal now isn't really the time. Do you think they saw us coming in here? I don't know "Anna", but we should be ready for a fight just to be safe, and find a place to hide in case they come in we wouldn't be able to take them on in a fair fight, so we need to use a little bit of stealth and take them on one by one from the shadows. Okay and we should probably be really quite. Search the city take what you can and feed on the helpless ones. Yes sir. Hey daddy maybe we can search that cathedral and search for those two I saw flee in here when we were flying over the city. No! "Cassandra" we are not searching for them. One of them looked like lord Althezed's banished daughter. Did she now well that changes everything now doesn't it? So we can search for them then daddy? Fine just be careful the lords daughter isn't without training in the way of the sword she won't be an easy win if that's what you were hoping for. She's just a little shrimp how could she beat me? That right there is going to be your downfall you underestimate your opponent and that's why you will not win. What do you mean I'm a great fighter how could she beat me? Like I said that is going to be your down fall you think she's weak so she will win against you in a fight. Fine I'll be careful is that better? Take a few men with you.

Ah fine "Kane, Larz, Kale, Elson" you're with me. Yes ma'am we are searching the cathedral. Yes we are searching for "Lennzie" and her little friend as well. Ok "Anna" get ready for a fight they are getting ready to come in be very careful. Ok "Lennzie" I'll be ready for them. Shush their almost here. Little vampire come out, come out wherever you are. Come out "Lennzie" I know you're here, you two check over there. "Anna" get ready to strike if you find a small opening take it. Ah Shink Thud. Ah Shink Thud. Now there's only three left, and we will need to fight them. Ah "Lennzie" there you are you will come with me, or your death will be utmost slow and painful. I'm not going anywhere with you or your fang bitten crew, not even over my dead body. That can be arranged for you. No! We need her alive for now or it will be you who dies. But she's going to die anyways. Who... Who...Are you? Great "Jarred" you finally caught up with us what took you so long? No time to talk about that right now "Lennzie". Fine for now we fight "Anna" you take him, "Jarred" you got him and that leaves this fang bitten slug brain for me. Mouse girl this won't hurt a bit I'll give you a quick death. Your right this won't hurt me but it will hurt you. You're just a weak little baby. Ha. Ha. Ha. Ha I'm not a baby! Swish, Swish, Clang, Clang, Dodge, Dodge, Clang, Clang, Ahhhhh how! How could I lose to a baby mouse girl? Hey "Lennzie" when did she learn to fight like that? Man I really must have been gone for a while. Yeah it's been two years six months and four days bird beak not like any monster was counting or anything. Yea I missed you too "Lennzie" and your humor as well. Never mind that right now bird beak. Okay have it your way little ms fang tooth. Okay let us fight "Lennzie" just you and me. Bring it on fang twit I can beat you with one arm tied behind my back. Well let's see about that shall we? Yes we shall Swish, Swish, Clang, Clang, Dodge, Clang, Dodge Ahhh. How? How could I lose to a little shrimp like you? I'm not a shrimp! Ahhh how could I lose to a were bird! No! Well that went well. Mhahahahahahahhahaha silly "Lennzie" did you really think you could hide from me? Who said I was hiding? What's that supposed to mean. It means fang lip I was trying to draw you in, I saw you flying into this city and I hid in here to draw you into me, that's why I also stopped in the graveyard to grab this. Getting you to come to me seems to have worked out better than I thought it would. What? So you wanted me to find you? See you do catch on quickly bug brain. Why let me catch you? Catch me? You catch me! You think I let you find me to catch me? If you didn't let me catch you then why did you let me find you then? I drew you in because I need someone to tell my dad I'm fighting in this war. How did you know we didn't have orders to kill you on sight? If you were here to kill me you would have done it by now, you're also just a scout and from what I heard your orders were to bring me back alive, now that's really got to make you mad. Well looks like those orders may have changed yes I do believe they did it would be an honor to kill her. You however need to return to my father, I'll kill her. Tell my father his will be done. Yes princess I'll take my leave. Good now that she's gone, what do you want "Devli'anna" and why are you here. Hold up I'm not who you think I am see. Who are you? I believe the monster that just saved your skins. Yes but who are you? I'm a shape-shifter my name is "Azzed", I'm not just one monster or another but I can be any monster I want whenever I want I don't really have a gender role either. Well "Azzed" thanks for saving our skins but I think we should head out before she returns. Yes great plan "Jarred" but may I remind you I can't travel in sunlight. Sunlight won't kill you would it "Lennzie"? No "Azzed" it won't kill me if I am in it for short periods of time, but it will burn a lot but if I'm in the sun for a long time I can die from that and I really don't want to turn to ashes. Well there's some old tapestry hanging up maybe you could use that as a way to shield yourself from the sun until we can find a better cloak for you to use. Or she could turn into a bat and ride in the back sack I found. Yes "Anna" that is a great idea let's do that it will also save us some time. We should head out now, and we are off. Hey

"Azzed" where are we going? Anywhere but here because if we stay here we are as good as dead. Okay so we are out of this place then we can head out-of-the city now. I was starting to think they would never leave. "Me too' Solthes" but it's a good thing "Azzed" got here in time to help them. Yes "Althes" but how are we going to? Shush we aren't supposed to speak of that, but I don't know yet, maybe we will know when the time is right but for now we just keep doing the same thing we've been doing, for now for it's not time yet for us to play a big role in things just yet. Yes "Althes" but what about the soul gems do you think they can really bring them back? Shush we aren't supposed to talk about that but yes they will but that isn't what we need to worry about right now, but that is something for another time. You know, we can't talk about those things why did you ask about it? I'm sorry I just wanted to know your thoughts. Yes I know what you mean and yes it is something we need to think about, I know, but we must not think on it too much it's not our place to do so. However, we can say this there're more friends and foes to come. Yes there will be I can't wait to see when they come. 'Me too "Solthes" me too, but enough with our riddles for now let's let them get back to "Anna, Lennzie" and the rest of the group to see how their travels are going so far. Hey "Lennzie" how are you doing back there? It's a bit bumpy back here but pretty good so far how about you "Anna"? I'm doing well a bit sweaty but good, how about you "Jarred"? I'm good a bit hot but well, what about you "Azzed"? I'm doing well, looks like our trip was shorter than we thought, or we didn't notice how long it really took us, looks like we are coming up on a small town. Hello strangers what brings you young folks out here to our town of Salezzed? We are trying to follow the group of vampires that attacked the city not far from here and they came through this way. So that's what all the ruckus was about then? No matter you can find plenty of Food, Water, Shelter, and much more in our little town. Thank you ma'am, but we can't take your money. Nonsense it's not my money a friend of yours left it with me to give you here's the six thousand lizards teeth for you to buy anything you need and more. Thank you ma'am. Please call me "Sondra". Thank you "Sondra" for the lizard's teeth, but if we are all here who is this friend that left this for us? I can't really tell you much they were tall and talked in riddles and babble talk. Thank you again "Sondra". Your very welcome youngins, oh and you the young blonde one may I talk with you alone for a minute please? Yes what is it? Your friend also gave me these to give to you as well and told me to make sure they went to you and only you, they also said you will need them where you will be going, but they didn't say where it was you would or why you would need them. They also said to make sure you keep them hidden and to tell you not to tell anyone about them; keep them safe youngin don't tell anyone about them. I won't tell anyone about them but why will I need them, and where will I be going to need them, more importantly what do they do? That your friend didn't say but I'm sure you will find out in good time young one. Okay "Sondra" thank you for giving us the lizards teeth and giving me these, I'll keep them safe. Hey "Lennzie" 'what did "Sondra" want to talk to you about? It went well thanks, hey we should stock up on supplies while we are here. Hey "Anna" mind if I take some lizards teeth to get a cloak and a mask so I can travel with the rest of you guys. Sure we have more than enough for you to take a bit, here take five hundred lizards teeth, we can each get five hundred lizards teeth, and still have plenty to get what we need. We should all meet back here when we are done with getting what we need before heading out of town. I'm going to try and see if I can find a cloak and mask for myself over there at that shop over there meet up with you guys soon. You might want to buy a mask for your face as well if you can so your face doesn't burn in the sun. Ouch that sounds like it would be very painful. Yes "Azzed" it is very painful it's one of the most painful things a vampire can feel. Really ouch that must really have to hurt then. Yeah but for now I'm going to try and find a cloak and a mask for myself. I'll meet you guys back here when we are all done getting what we need. We will meet up here on our way out-of-town see you guys in a bit. Now where to look for a cloak and mask? You could try that old magic shop over there. Okay thanks stranger. Please call me "Sizzes". I'll go check out the magic shop now. Hello stranger what brings you to the magic owl today? I was looking for a cloak and a face mask for vampires do you have one? I don't however a stranger did stop in here not too long ago and gave me these to give to you if that helps? Yes this works great thank you it's exactly what I was looking for thank you. Don't thank me thank your friend for leaving it here for you. Who was this friend anyways? I don't really know a mysterious fellow speaking riddles. Yea that sounds like them here let me give you three hundred lizard teeth for them. No keep it's an honor to give it to you. Okay well thank you again for holding on to this for me. Any time and you're welcome I hope you have a great day now. You as well it was nice meeting you. Hey "Lennzie" any luck with your mask and cloak? Yea I found these; any luck with food and water? Yeah we did we have food and water to last us a while. That's good we shouldn't die of heat sickness now. Hey does anyone else feel like some monster is watching over us? Not really. What about you "Jarred" or you "Anna" do you feel like some monster watching over us? Yea kind of. Yeah me too, but what if some monster really is watching over us? I have a hunch on who it could be. Yea who do you think it is? Oh nothing just thinking out loud I guess. We should get going we still have a long road ahead of us. We should get going then. Hey "Azzed" where are we off too now? I don't know, I don't even know how I got here I was spying on a castle next thing I knew I was saving you guys. So you don't even know how you got here? No I have no clue how I got here or why I was sent to save you guys, but either way it seems like I made it just in time to save you. You can't save me forever no one can. What do you mean by that? It means one day I will die no matter what you do to save me I will die, no matter what you do one day I will die. I can say this though if I die don't go fighting or killing to avenge my death, but live and fight to stay alive. "Lennzie" why are you talking like that? Because it's going to happen one day and no one will be able to save me. You are talking like you're going to die soon. We should get some rest looks like there's a cave up ahead. Good we can make camp there for the night. Yes we can set up camp here and head out in the morning we should also make some food; we have fire wood, a small pot to cook in and some fresh veggies and small supplies. Sounds good we could use a good meal and then get some shut-eye. I'll get a fire started in a small hole I dug in the dirt and work on getting a fire ready for us to cook on. We will work on cutting up the veggies and potatoes to go in the soup. Looks like we are all ready to put everything in the pot now all we need to do is add the water and put the pot on the fire and let it cook, it might take a while so if we fall asleep we can eat before heading out in the morning. Now that we got the soup on the fire if we want to get some sleep we can. It looks like they got the gifts we left for them just fine. Yes but I think we've helped them on their journey more than enough for now though. What about Lennzie? Do you think she knows more then she lets on or more then she lets the others know? Maybe or maybe us giving her those stones might have given her some insight on things as well. Do you think she knows what the stones are? We should believe she does she seems to know more then we think she does. I think there is more to "Lennzie" then meets the eye, there is probably more to her than we probably know about. I can say their travels are far from being over, and soon new travels will start. You weren't supposed to say that, but yes their travels have just truly gotten started and new travels are yet to come for a few of our friends. There is much in store on the path ahead. Yes new friends, more foes, and much more on the path ahead but for now we are off. Take it we are off to the same place we are always off to? They will be waking up soon and we are off. Good morning every monster. Good morning "Anna, Jarred, Lennzie". Morning to you "Jarred, Anna, and Azzed". Let's have some of that soup before we head out. We are going to need our strength for the long road ahead of us. Hey "Lennzie" you're going to need to wear your cloak and mask today it's also going to be really hot and sunny out today. Thank you for the heads up "Anna" how did you sleep last night? I slept pretty good how did you sleep? I slept ok I guess but you should probably eat before we have to head out. Yes that sounds good I'm going to need all the strength I can get as well, hopefully our travels go well again today. Me too but only time will say for sure. That's so true "Anna". Hey "Azzed" any idea where this road will take us? No I have no clue, but we should follow it and see where it goes. Okay let's follow the road and see where it takes us today and see what we find on the road ahead. Hey "Azzed", "Anna" where are you guys from? I come from a small group of shape-shifters. What about you "Anna"? I've lived in a few big open hollow trees, and a few caves, anywhere I could rest my head for a night or two. What about you "Lennzie"? I'm from a castle far to the north but I never really knew anywhere else until I had to start sleeping in caves and that's when "I met 'you and "Jarred". Yeah I remember that day too "Lennzie". Well looks like we came across another small town. Yea it looks that way and looks like it might be in chaos. This looks like a vampire raid, from the looks the raid happened overnight and seems like some monster might have been trying to set up a trap for us. Well that would explain the screaming and crying. What should we do then? We should be ready for a fight just in case they are still here. Good call be ready for anything, if they were attacked by vampires they could still be here. But "Lennzie" how could they still be here in day light? You see those tents? Yeah why? They can hide in the tents and lay in wait under the sand and wait for us to go into the tent and strike us from below like a trapdoor spider. Dang good thing you're on our side then you seem to know a lot about their attack style. Yes I've had my fair share of attacks and hunting you pick up and learn a few ways to keep what you're hunting from getting away. We need to try and find a building up off the ground and camp out there it doesn't seem like there's any safe ways out of the town from here. What the "Lennzie" look out Ha that was close. I told you it seemed like the way out of town was too dangerous to try and get out of town. Yes but how are they getting around in day light? They are underground hello. Yes but if they come up they burn in the sunlight right? Not going to be that easy with them they are also wearing masks and cloaks, they also seem to be using razor claws to attack us from below. They destroyed the town what else do they want? Well with the way they attacked us isn't it obvious what they want? Why would they attack us we don't have anything that they would want? They want me; they want to take me to my father for the blood moon on the rise. The way they came after us seems like they were also trying to kill "Azzed". What do we do then? No matter what happens to me watch over "Anna". "Anna" you and "Jarred" watch over "Azzed" do what you can to keep him safe. Hey "Anna, Jarred" promise me no matter what happens to me don't fight to avenge what happens to me, fight to stay alive don't fight to avenge me. Yes we promise "Lennzie" we will fight to survive we will fight only when we have to. We will also protect "Azzed" I will try and distract the others if they are focused on me you should be able to try and get out of town. What if they catch you "Lennzie" we can't just leave you behind you're a part of this group we're not going to just leave you behind. I need to do this if you stay we will all die, if I stay you have a chance to find somewhere safe. With this open area they will over power all of us if you control the battle field you could fight them, leave me and protect "Azzed". We will, but we are also going to protect you as well we're not leaving you behind "Lennzie" you are a part of this group; and we aren't leaving you alone we protect each other remember, we are also a team. "Anna's" right we won't let you go down this path alone "Lennzie". I didn't ask you to let me, but I have to do this I know it doesn't make sense to you but you need to trust me on this. I'm not gonna lose you "Lennzie" I'm not leaving you behind. Anna! I need to do this, just because we are saying goodbye doesn't mean its goodbye forever. But....But "Lennzie" I need you. "Anna" you have "Jarred" and "Azzed" to guide you for now. "Anna" I'm scared enough as it is don't make this harder for me, I have to do this, this isn't the end I will be back one day. Hey if you two are done talking we are under attack. Kill the shape-shifter and bring "Lennzie" to lord Althezed alive for now. Yes sir. Hey "Lennzie" how many are there? Six maybe more I can't really say but I can say they out number us. They can take me as long as "Anna" makes it out-of-town safe. It might not be what you want to hear but it's better than us fighting blind. That's true this will have to work we can't be picky we will fight the best we can with what we have. No matter what happens to me don't come looking for me "Anna" promise me you won't try to look for me. Okay "Lennzie" I promise I won't go looking for you. Sorry "Lennzie" we can't just leave you to your fate. I'm not asking you to I'm telling you to go on without me. Why do you have to go? Because it's my fate. That's all you can say is that it's your fate to go with them? Yes. All I can say is it's my fate for whatever happens. Fine we won't go looking for you, however they won't be taking you without a fight. Speaking of why haven't they attacked us yet? It's almost night fall what are they waiting for? Oh no it's a few nights early why is it a few nights early? What is it "Lennzie" A Blood moon is on the rise. What does that have to do with you? Because...Because it's the moon I was born under and it's the moon where I die and no one can save me. "Lennzie", no it can't be true. It is true "Jarred" don't try to save me, I will be back again. Fight on without me for now. What do you mean you will be back one day and fight on without you for now? That I can't say I just really need you to trust me on this I can't say how I know this but I just do you just have to trust me. Okay "Lennzie" I have faith in you, you can do this I don't know what this is but I have faith you can do this "Lennzie". Thanks "Jarred" that means a lot to me. You know me bird beak I'll come out on top as well. You will be missed by us as well even more so by

"Anna", she will take you being gone the hardest of us all, she cares about you very much, maybe even loves you so your being gone is really going to take a toll on her. I know can you do me a favor and keep an eye on "Anna" for me while I'm gone. Yes I can do that for you "Lennzie". Thank you bird beak I'll see you again soon. Nice to see even with staring death in the face you still have your sense of humor intact. Well hello this is me you're talking about. Yeah I forgot who I was talking to little ms fang tooth. Ha-Ha speaking of why haven't they attacked us yet? It seems like they are waiting for some monster but whom? If they are waiting for some monster chances are they are waiting on my father to get here, they could also be trapping us until my dad gets here. Why would they do that if they can fight us why trap us in here? Because what better way to kill your prey then to trap it in a corner and make it think it has a chance to get away and then spring the trap and kill the prey. Wow "Lennzie" you know a lot about this don't you. I've had my fair share of hunts. Um guys its night fall and they should be coming up from underground any second now. Protect "Azzed" with everything you have. What about you "Lennzie". No it's my time…It's my time but it's not the end. What do you mean it's not the end? That I can't say but you just need to trust me "Azzed". Fine I trust you. Thank you all for your support I'll miss you guys while I'm gone. We are going miss you while you're gone "Lennzie". But we will fight on without you for now. Blood on a full moon you better fight on without me. Um guys its night fall and a blood moon fills the sky. Oh yea, and we are under attack just so you know. Lord Althezed they are in there sir. Excellent they are right where we want them kill the shape-shifter and bring "Lennzie" to me. Capture the other two I want them to watch their friend die before we kill them. Yes sir. "Salzed" bring six men with you they won't come without a fight. Yes sir you heard him men six of you come with me. Well….Well if it isn't "Lennzie" you're coming with us. Yeah I'll go with you but I won't go easy. Finally, some action "Anna, Jarred, Azzed" now! Thud Thud now it's my turn to bring you to our lordship Althezed. "Lennzie" you sure you don't want any help? No I've got this but thanks. You two attack her and bring her to lord Althezed alive. Yes sir. Bring it on bug brains I can take you both on at once. Dodge, Clang, Dodge, Clang, Dodge, Swish Thwack Thud. Lennzie! No! "Anna" she's not dead she knocked out. You two are about to join her. Ahhhhh "Azzed" No! Thud Jarred! You're next. I don't think so you fang bitten death breathe. Swish Thud. Silly little girl did you really think you could best a vampire during a full blood moon. Huh! What happened? My head hurts? What happened? We three are captives and "Azzed" is dead. When? Right before we got knocked out "Anna". What about "Lennzie" is she okay? Me? Why don't you open your eyes "Anna" and see for yourself. There you are "Lennzie". Geesh "Anna" you're so blind. Ha-Ha "Lennzie" I was just knocked out I couldn't see you at first. "Anna" you are too silly Ha-Ha-Ha. How interesting you face death in the face yet here you are cracking jokes. Hello dad you of all people should know that about me. Huh yes I shouldn't be but you never did cease to amaze me yet again there's more to you than meets the eye. Maybe there is maybe there isn't but it's not like you will ever know. What's that supposed to mean? Oh nothing...nothing you don't need to worry about that. I'll give you a slow painful death. Ha-Ha do your worst. As you wish "Lennzie". Ha no weapons? No need for that I can crush you without them, I can crush you with my mind. Ha.Ha. Huh? Ahhhhhhhh! What's he doing to her! He's killing her with his mind "Anna". Anna! Jarred! Fight till the end! "Anna" I won't forget you! Lennzie! I won't forget you either I will fight on until the end! "Anna" I'll always be in your heart. I love you! I love you too Lennzie! Oh how sweet it'll be her love for your friendship with you that gets you killed. No! Noooooooooooooooooooooooooo! Ahhhhhhhhhh! Ahhhhhhhh! Crunch! Snap! Lennzie! Noooooooo! Thud. Lennzie! Noooo! You're gonna pay for that you hear me you're gonna pay! Ahhh! Crunch! Thud. Jarred! Ha-Ha What.....What's this power? Sir I think it's coming from her sir. Huh what's this! You won't use that move to hurt any monster ever again! Not me, not the poor town folks you killed, not my friends, not any monster! Thud. Thud. Thud. Thud. Thud. Thud. How? How is she killing of our men? What the..... how? How is she making weapons out of nothing and killing us? Retreat before she kills us all. My lord we need to get out of here. Ahhh! Thud. Thud. Fine we retreat for now but mock my words mouse girl you will die! Ahhh! Ahhh! Thud. Thud. Ha-Ha-Ha I live thud. Oh great she's passed out. Yes but she needs her rest after what she just did. There's no doubt now she is the legendary oracle. So it's a good thing we made the right choice to train her then. It also looks like our beloved friends have been sent on their way and started their new journey. Ah yes it seems they have, we will see them again soon. Yes you are right about that they will be back sooner than we think. I wonder how our friends are doing on their travels so far. As do I, but we can't travel there, yet we will keep an eye on "Anna" for now and see how she's doing we will check on our beloved friends in good time. But for now we are going to make sure she is still alive before we go; are we going to undo her bindings before leave our friend. Oh my head is killing me where is every monster? Oh no Jarred? Lennzie? Wake up we have to get away from here. Come on guys please wake up. Jarred? Lennzie? Wake up we have to go. They are dead my friend. No! They can't be dead you're lying! Look at them! They aren't even breathing "Anna". How do you know my name? Who are you? I heard you talking to your friends, my name is "Alezalifed" but you can call me "Al" for it's easier than trying to say my name. I am a shadow walker. What is a shadow walker? A shadow walker is neither alive nor dead, they send their souls to search for things without getting in harm's way and can find a safe path to where they are trying to reach, they can travel to purgatory and beyond as well but it's not easy though; I'm male I'm also Gay but it's okay. I'm Transgender so I won't judge you. Thank you "Anna" you are a really good monster I'm so sorry about your friends.

Thank you that means a lot to me, you are also a good monster as well "Al". "Anna" we should get out of here. Yes but I'm going to bury my friends first, I can't leave them like this. That's an honorable thing you are doing for your friends. I can help you bury them if I may. Yes you can help and thank you for helping me. No problem "Anna" I'm just glad I could help you honor your fallen friends. Okay we're just about done here that went faster than I thought it would. Yeah it's faster when you have more than one monster working on it. That's true have you had to do this before? Yes many times during times of war. I'm so sorry "Al" that must have been hard on you? Thanks yes it was very hard on me at first but it also got easier over time. Do you think I'll ever get over this? No but I think it will get easier as time goes on, the truth is I can't really answer that for you it's something that you can only answer for yourself in time. I also believe you will see your friends again soon. How do you know that? Because I have faith that they are working on a way to see you again. Yeah I guess you're right I can put faith into that. Hey "Al" where do you think our path will take us? I hope it takes us to a utopia where all monsters are free to be themselves and not be made fun of or abandoned for being Gay, Lesbian, Transgender, Bi, or None-gender. A utopia we can all be a part of sounds amazing a place where we can always be safe with friends all around us; having friends does have a nice ring to it. Some monsters tell me it's just a silly dream what do you think "Anna"? I don't think it's a silly dream I'd love a place like that for me and my friends to live in peace. Do you think we will find a monster utopia at the end of our journey? I think it could happen I think we will also have more battles to fight along the way. I've been to a place and where there were other monsters, and we had a school I had only been to once or twice. Wow how was school when you went? It was fun I had a great time there, there was a music school for monsters, but I think we have come across a forest. A forest in the desert seems a little odd don't you think no it's more common than you might think. How so; how many are there? There are two that I know about theirs wolf den woods, and then there's bloodbath forest. Oh both have such charming names which one do you think we are at, we don't have to go through there do we? Unfortunately we do but if we stay awake and keep our eyes open we should be able to make it through without much fuss, we also won't be stopping until we get to whatever's on the other side. Yes I wouldn't want to stick around and find out where it gets its name from. Well wolf den woods gets its name from a clan of Werewolves that lives there, bloodbath forest gets its name from all the blood spilt there during many wars long ago now its home to a bunch of blood thirsty creatures. What types of creatures live in there do you think we will come across anything going through the forest? We could face Demons, Ghouls, Goblins, Fairies, and more in there if we are alone or asleep in there we are dead. How do we kill what's in there do you know? We don't however I do have my blessed beads that should help keep them at bay for a while as long as my light shines bright. Sounds good if we can't kill them it's better to keep them away from us. That's the plan let's just hope it works if it doesn't well no worries. No worries why no worries? Because if doesn't work we will both be dead that's why I said no worries. Oh well no worries we can make it through. Yeah what makes you say that? Just a feeling I have. Either way we are on our way through the forest oh and keep this close to you at all times it will keep you safe. This will keep us safe and keep me safe? It will as long as we believe it will the more you believe in it the more it will protect you and ward those nasty things off from making you their next meal. I have faith this will protect us and keep us safe. We are heading into the woods now so be on guard. This forest looks amazing. Yes it can be it shows us things that aren't real to try and get our guard down in this place. Because everything in here would kill you if given half a chance. I'll be careful that I can do. Help! Help me! Wait "Al" do you hear that? We can't trust it. We can't ignore it either what if some monster really is in trouble they need our help. I'm not helping them. Fine I'll go help them then have fun being all alone. "Anna"? "Anna"! Ah dark shadows help us she doesn't get us both killed. "Anna" wait I'm coming with you. Help! Help me! Who's screaming for help? No clue but we should be coming up on them soon. I see that it looks like an elf. Blood shadows what's an elf doing in here? I could ask the same question about you two, if I had to guess. My name's "Salevi'anna" what's your name? My name is "Alezalifed" but you can call me "Al". My name is "Anna". So you're what all the fuss was about back there? So you've heard of me? I've heard rumors some small talk about the one to end the rule of vampires in these parts. What do these rumors say about me? Think you can get me out of this trap first please. Yes we can get you out of this trap. Thank you "Anna" here "Anna" I want you to have this it's an Elfish necklace of protection it will ward evil away from you and keep you safe. It also shields you from anything evil it keeps them from getting to close to you as well. Wow that's cool. It's way more effective then that make shaft blessed bead light, this will protect you for close to forever unlike that blessed bead light that's starting to die we should get out of here now. What are you saying about my blessed bead light? Nothing I'm just surprised it's kept you safe this long even though its light is dying out. Ah shadow fain she's right let's get out of here before Demons, Fairies, and more come swarming on this spot looking to eat us. "Al's" right we need to get out of here. Let's go this way to get out of here, so what brings you and a shadow walker to these parts anyway? Me and my friends were attacked by vampires the same vampires killed my friends and I passed out, the vampires that attacked us were also part my friends family. When I came to my senses there were dead vampires all around me. You survived it how? They never leave any monster alive from their raids. I don't know how I survived I passed out and must have scared them off or something. No don't look at me that was all you "Anna" when you passed out you ended up taking out a handful of vampires while tied up weapons started coming out of nowhere and vampires were dying like you had swatted a fly. When I finally got to "Anna" I thought she was dead until she started to move. Sounds like she is very lucky to be alive. She's very lucky no monster has ever survived a vampire attack like the one you and your friends went through. Yes I guess you're right no monster has ever survived before, no one but "Anna" that is. I'm very sorry about your friend's "Anna". Thanks "Salevi'anna" that means a lot to me. Please call me "Sal". I'm thankful to still be alive. You should show your friends they didn't die in vain. What like revenge? I made a promise to a friend before she died that I wouldn't revenge her death but fight to stay alive. So you won't kill your friend's killer because of a promise you made. Yes and I plan to honor my promise to her if her killer tries to come after me I will fight to stay alive; but I won't do it for revenge nothing you say or doing is going to make me break that promise I made to her. You're honoring your friends dying wishes I can respect that you're right to honor your friends dying wish. It was your friends dying wish that you only fight to stay alive I honor your loyalty to your friend. We are safely out of the forest now and should find a place to rest for a while before we go any farther. After that back there we shouldn't have any issue getting any rest. Goodnight "Al" good night "Sal". Goodnight "Anna", goodnight to you "Al". No! Lennzie! No! Jarred! No! Lennzie! I love you! Jarred! No! Lennzie! No! "Anna"! "Anna" wake up you're safe go back to sleep I'll keep you safe. Thank you for keeping me safe "Sal". You're welcome "Anna" sleep now Shhhhh. Shhhhhh sleep now I'll hold you and keep you safe. Looks like "Anna's" nightmares have started already; this isn't the first time this has happened remember. Yes but that's for another story for another time. Yes your right, "Anna" seems to be doing as well as can be expected for what she's been through. She would have probably died if it wasn't for our training. Maybe but she did pull off something even we didn't teach her. Ah yes that is true what she did even we can't explain how it happened, but she is alive, so we can't really expect much more than that from her for right now. Even the secrete move we showed her has nothing on the one she did I believe if we didn't train her at all we might be having a different talk then the one we are having right now. Yes maybe but enough of us they will be waking up soon. Good morning "Anna", good morning "Al". Good morning "Sal", good morning "Anna". Where are we off to today? I think we should stay here for a few nights to figure things out.

To be continued.

Origins of Lennzie / Origins of Anna / Journey through Purgatory

Origins of Lennzie

"**M**y name"... "My name is Lennzie." I am the fourth child born to my mother "Salo'vonna" and my father lord Althezed. But my story starts at my birth, for without me being born there can't really be any story about me can there. Vampires don't just fall from the sky you know. But where was I again? Oh-Oh yeah I was talking about the day I was born. It was a dark summer night on a full blood moon I was born. My sisters weren't happy about my birth." momma" why do we need another sister? "Rachel" your father and I wanted another child. "But"... But "momma" it's not fair. It's not up to you about what's fair or not "Devili'anna" just because your mother and I had another child. Doesn't mean we love you any less. Doesn't mean we have to lover her. Well you should she is your sister whether you like it or not, she shares the same blood line as you. "Well we could always eat her." No! "Sali'zanna" you can't eat your sister. You are not eating your sister "Lennzie". Oh great you named it! Before it showed up you let us eat whoever we wanted to. Enough! You can eat each other for all I care just leave your baby sister out of it. Fine but it's not like we wanted her here anyways, and you can't make us like her. Girls! That's enough from you now go your rooms. But "daddy" do we have to go to our rooms? Yes "Devili'anna" you have to go to your rooms. You and momma don't care about us anymore now that it was born. Your mother and I still love all of you "Sali'zanna" all four of you. This stinks! I can always lock you in the prison cells with no blood or any way to feed and see just how unfair I can really be. You wouldn't do that to us we are your daughters. So is "Lennzie", so do you choose your rooms or prison cells. Fine we will go to our rooms but know we go in protest. You can protest all you want you are not eating your sister "Lennzie". We are off to our rooms; we still don't see why you had to name it. Silence! Now go. Fine girls let's go maybe we can find some monster to eat on our way to our rooms. Don't you fear "Lennzie" daddy is watching over you, no one will harm you while I'm around. "Althezed" hun "Lennzie" and I need some rest it's been a long night and it's going to be an even longer day. Are you sure you don't need me for anything "Salo'vonna"? Yes I'm sure go check on the girls and make sure they haven't eaten anyone they shouldn't. If you're sure you don't need me I'm off. If I needed you I wouldn't be telling you to leave. True...True I'm off take care my love. You take care as well my love, don't think too harshly of the girls they are not used to the idea of having another sister. For our sake and "Lennzie's" I hope your right. Sleep easy "Lennzie" daddy will take care of you; I'm off to make sure the girls aren't doing anything they shouldn't. Remember don't think too harshly of them dear. I won't. Now "Lennzie" it's just "you 'and mommy" now just know mommy loves you very much, and I will be watching over you always. Always remember mommy loves you "Lennzie" mommy loves you always. This is where my story starts at my birth and the death of my mother, and the beginning of my life as a vampire. Now we can skip ahead in time to my fifth birthday. Hey "Lennzie" happy birthday little sister how are you on this fine day. You know very well how I'm feeling "Rachel" we go through this every year. Yes we do you know why? Because you're a two faced fang twit that blames me for mom's death. You best believe I blame you for mom's death if her and daddy didn't have you she would still be alive. "Rachel" that's enough you know very well it wasn't your sister's fault your mother died. But daddy it's her fault mom's dead. No it's not and you know it, your mother had a hole in her heart, and she was going to die anyways, and she wanted to have your sister before she died. Yeah well if you and mom didn't have her she would still be here right now. You know that's not true now leave your sister be. But daddy. I said go or do you need some time in the prison cells to cool down. No I'm good I'll leave her be for now. Good now get out of here you two faced fang twit. Why you little. "Rachel" that's enough! Now leave us. I'll leave you and little Ms Baby fang alone for now see you later baby sister. "Well that went well" happy birthday hunny how's your birthday going so far all things considered. It's going pretty good I guess. I love you "Lennzie". I love you to daddy. I hope your birthday has been going well all things considered. Oh yes I still need to meet up with "Ly'anna". Sounds like fun I won't keep you have fun with your visit with "Ly'anna", don't stay out to late I have something I want to give you later when you get back. "Ly'anna" I made it where are you? Ooof "Ly'anna" why did you jump on me? Why not silly Lennzie head you make a great landing pad. How's your birthday going? Eh you know same thing different sister. Who is it this time? Just "Rachel" blaming me for my mom's death again as always. I'm sorry your sisters do that to you every year on your birthday. It's not your fault but thank you, my sisters have hated me since the day I was born. That's not cool, but at least you have me Lennzie head. Yeah and you always seem to know what to say to cheer me up and make me smile. That's my job silly it also helps I know you better than most vampires. True and I love spending time with you. "How long have we been hanging out for?" at least four years or so why? Well how else do you think I know you so well Lennzie head? Yeah I guess you're right about that. Of course I'm right like a vampire bite. Oh "Ly'anna" you always cheer me up. Of course I do silly "Oh yeah" before I forget I have this to give you before you go. "Ly'anna"...It's....It's beautiful I love it. I'm glad you love it I saw it and thought you just had to have it. Well I have to go have fun with your dad "Lennzie" mah. "Ly'anna" you kissed my cheek. Mah that better Lennzie head your face was made for my kisses. Yeah I know, but we can't let anyone catch us either. Why? We just love each other why is that so wrong? I wish I knew the answer to that as well. I love you "Ly'anna" and I always will. I will always love you to "Lennzie" and I always will. See you again soon mah I love you "Lennzie". Oh and happy birthday again. Thanks again for the gift "Ly'anna" I love it. You're welcome Lennzie head I'm glad you love it night. Night "Ly'anna". Daddy there you are. How did your visit with "Ly'anna" go? It went well she also gave me this. Well isn't that nice, I'm glad you and "Ly'anna" had a great visit. You also said you had something you wanted to give me. Yes this was your mother's she would have wanted you to have this. Daddy it's beautiful I love it, thank you very much daddy. You are very welcome "Lennzie" I'm glad you love it. I love you sweet heart it's going to be morning soon, and we should get some rest for tomorrow is going be a long night. Goodnight daddy I love you. Now that we have that out of the way let's jump ahead in time to when I turned nine. No don't worry it's not another birthday memory just one of those good days I had before everything went wrong in my life. Hey "Lennzie" you want to go play in the garden and the graveyard? Yeah "Ly'anna" that would be awesome, you know I love playing in the garden and the graveyard. Yeah I know but I still like to ask you any ways. Yeah we should get heading we have to be back before sun rise. Okay Lennzie head did you want to play in the garden and then play in the graveyard? Let's play in the garden first. Okay Lennzie head let's get going then. Ok "Ly'anna" lead the way. Or how about you come and walk next to me. I can do that and then

I can do this. Silly Lennzie head that tickles. Your hand was made for my hand silly "Ly'anna". Ha-Ha very funny Lennzie head. Yeah but you know you love me. Yep you're right like a vampire bite on that one. We aren't far from the garden now you want to race to the garden. Oh you are so on slow poke. You are so on Lennzie head. On your mark get set go. Ha-Ha-Ha-Ha... I'm gonna beat you there. Ha-Ha-Ha-Ha not a chance slow poke I got you beat on this one. That's what you think Lennzie head. Ha ooof "Ly'anna" you jumped on me. Yep you're made to be my landing pad mah you know you love me though. Well yeah I'm always going love you mah I love you to. So you wanna play hide-and-seek or werewolf and prey? Werewolf and prey I love that game. Yes werewolf and prey is a great game, I'll be the werewolf and you can be the prey Lennzie head. Okay just give me a small head start. That's fine I'm a werewolf and werewolves love fast food. Ha-Ha-Ha-Ha well just try and catch me slow poke. You are so on prey, oh "Lennzie" I'm going to find you my prey. I got you! Ooof "Ly'anna" how did you find me so fast? It wasn't really that hard I just followed the growling. Growling what growling? If that growling wasn't you "Lennzie" and it wasn't me. "Ly'anna" I think it's time we get back to the castle now. Wait "Ly'anna" do you hear that whistling sound? Cross bow shot "Ly'anna" hit the ground now! Zip! Aroo Thud. Princess "Lennzie" 'you and "Ly'anna" need to get back to the castle now it's not safe for you two to be out here, we are under attack by werewolves. Come on "Ly'anna" let's get going we have to run back to the castle. "Oh" and thank you for saving us from those werewolves. Don't thank us thank your sisters for letting us know about the attack. "Lennzie" we should head back now. Yes you're right I also need to talk to my no good fang bitten sisters anyways. Let's go for now you can yell at your sisters after I leave. Aroo Thud. Yeah let's get going we need to run all the way back to the castle up for a little race back to the castle. Yeah "Lennzie" we can run now, and we can talk when we get back to the castle. That was a shorter run then it seemed. Okay now that we are safe we should probably check on your sisters and see if they are okay. I guess you're right we should probably check on my no good fang bitten sisters and see if they are okay. I know they haven't been the greatest to you but you should at least see if they are okay. Yeah you're probably right like usual. You bet your right fang I'm right silly. Besides I still need to yell at them for spying on us any ways. Come on my sisters bedrooms are down this way if they are here they will be in my sister "Rachel's" room, my sisters rooms are down this way and my room isn't far down the hallway from their rooms. Hey "Lennzie" I think one of those werewolves starched me. What? When? The one that landed at my feet while we were running back here I think it scratched me but in the mist of all the panic I didn't notice it until now. This is not good if anyone finds out about this you are as good as dead we need to try and find a way to hide this from any monster until we can find away to cure it. Yeah Lennzie head we should try and keep this to ourselves for the time being. Right my sisters usually hang out in here if they are here that is. Well girls look at who came to check on us to make sure we were okay. Shut it "Sali'zanna" we didn't come here to make small talk, why were you spying on "me 'and "Ly'anna" in the garden. That wasn't use we just got back from going hunting for food with dad, if you don't believe us you can even go ask him yourself. If you weren't spying on us in the garden, then who told the guards they were you and where "Lennzie" 'and me" were. We have no clue who or what told the guards they where us, or why they were spying on you. Whoever was spying on you must have known the guards wouldn't believe anyone else if they said werewolves were attacking the castle. Shut it you two faced fang twits if you didn't spy on us then who could have known about the attack on the castle. Those guards came just in time to save us from the werewolves that where in the garden. Well it wasn't us like we said we just got back from hunting with dad when you two showed up asking us about spying on our baby sister. Like "Rachel" was saying we were with daddy the whole time if you don't believe us you can just ask him when he gets back from fighting werewolves off our lands. Shut it "Devili'anna" I wasn't talking to you. Crash! The werewolves' seem to have breached the castle walls, we will go check on daddy you and your girlfriend stay here and protect the castle. Oh and "Ly'anna" you might want to see about some wolves bane for that scratch, if you get anymore scratches wolves bane won't be much help at that point. What are you talking about "Rachel"? Look at your leg if you really need a reminder. Hey if our sister's girlfriend turns into a vampire/werewolf she is going to die, or if she's lucky she will just die. But her being our sisters girlfriend she will have a double death, our dear sister will probably get banished from the castle. Gee thanks "Sali'zanna" you're so much help. You are very welcome my dear baby sister anything to help your girlfriend stay safe. What are you getting at "Sali'zanna"? I mean my lezbo sister we should keep her safe, so you can stay off our backs. I still remember what you did to that boy that one time he tried to bully "Ly'anna". Yeah no thank you I'm good as is thank you very much. Girls let's go check on daddy and leave these two love birds alone. See you later baby sister. Now that their gone we can speak freely. Sounds good to me, I never thought your sisters would treat you the way they do. Yeah they probably had you fooled because that's pretty much how they treat me all time. You should remember my sisters are two faced fang twits that will make themselves seem nice. I'm starting to see that I'm sorry they treat you like that. It's not your fault you didn't know; if I didn't know my sisters as well as I do, I wouldn't have thought they would do this me either. But they don't care about anything but each other and my father. Yeah I never thought they could be that cruel to you. Yeah well unless you see it for yourself it doesn't seem like they would ever treat me like that. They were cruel about our love as well why is our love so wrong to others. I wish I knew the answer but I don't know. I wish people would just let us love each other like every monster else, how does our relationship affect them. I wish I knew but I don't even know the answer to that. Crash! Werewolves! "Ly'anna" there're swords in a case under the bed take two swords and then pass two to me. Okay I think I found the swords. Yes they are inside that case. Crash! Smash! Uh "Ly'anna" not to rush you or anything but those swords would be really helpful right about now. Ah-Ha I got it here "Lennzie" catch. Arooo! Thud. "Ly'anna" look out behind you! Aroo! Thud. Thud. Wow "Ly'anna" how did you do that? I don't know I just reached out to attack those werewolves attacking me. Yeah you got them alright you struck out and killed them in one sword strike. Lennzie head you don't need to be afraid of me I would never hurt you. I think one of those werewolves' scratches changed me in some way. I think I'm starting to change "Lennzie" I think those other werewolves we fought scratched me. "Lennzie" promise me no matter what happens to me you will not revenge my death, no matter how I die do not revenge my death only kill to survive don't try to revenge my death. "Ly'anna" I promise you I will only fight to survive and I will not try to avenge your death. Lennzie head remember I love you always. I love you always to "Ly'anna". If word gets out about you being half vampire/half werewolf you will end up with a double death sentence. Lennzie head we can't hide this from every monster forever sooner or later they will find out about what I've become. We should be able to hide it for a bit, my scratch is just a scar now. Monsters will be coming back soon, so we should try and hide the scar for now. Now we will seal our promise with a pinky promise, I can keep my pinky promises. That's why we are doing our pinky promise. Wait do you hear that horn blowing? Yeah I hear it sounds like we have driven the werewolves away. Well look here girls look at who had a busy night. What are you getting at "Devili'anna" you two faced fang bitten fang twit? Just you killed all these werewolves, and yet "Ly'anna" is half vampire/ half werewolf, so she counts as a werewolf. So? That means you should have killed her with the rest of the mutts. Like any werewolf all a werewolves is, is just a mutt. She is already facing a double death sentence as it is one for being a werewolf and the other for being a Lesbian. We aren't going run away if that's what you are trying to say "Devili'anna". No it wouldn't help even if you did try and run away. Yeah I know that already "Rachel" thanks for the memo. Just reminding you dear baby sister of mine. Ha...Yeah right dear sister coming from you, yeah that's rich none of you three ever cared about me so why pretend you care about me now. No you're right there is no reason for us to start caring about you now, we can't wait for you to be gone. What did you do you no good fang bitten two faced fang twits do? We think you know exactly what we are talking about. You have got to be bloody kidding me! You didn't do what I think you did, did you? What we didn't tell daddy anything he didn't already know. What do you mean by that? Nothing just its daddy there's not much that goes on that he doesn't know about. What do you mean "Sali'zanna" you didn't play a hand in this at all? Just spill it out already. Fine you're going find out sooner or later anyways so might as well tell you, we told daddy about your love for each other and the werewolf scratch as well. You did what! I'm gonna. No... Lennzie head don't stoop down to their level. Yeah you're right I am better than them. They are no more than vampire ashes on full blood moon. If she's lucky maybe they might stick her in a cage, and treat her like the mutt she is now. How dare you say that about "Ly'anna" you have no right to talk about "Ly'anna" like that? You will find I can say what I want about whoever I want; I'd like to see you try and stop me. Come over here and I will you two faced fang twit. No baby sister I'm perfectly fine over here thanks. What are you scared? Scared? Me scared? No...No you're not scared of her; you're scared of me and the werewolf inside of me. No...I'm not scared of you what makes you think that. The way you keep hiding from me behind your sisters and your fear of werewolves. I don't know what you are talking about. You know exactly what I'm talking about; you always did like playing off anything you that scared you. That's not true. Girls enough! Yes...Yes daddy. Now let me handle things. Now you three be off now without another word. We will put her in the prison cells for now, the sun has come up we will take care of this later. "Ly'anna" has a double death sentence. Why does she have to die? She saved me from those werewolves. That is very nice but it's not going to help her case in any way. She is a werewolf, and she is a Lesbian, so she will die. So I'm her Lesbian lover what does that say about me? You are my daughter you will be lucky if you get banished. Why is her sentence harsher than mine? Because it's my ruling, what did you think I was going to kill you with your lover? So you are going to kill "Ly'anna" 'and banish me". Why does she have to die? She is not a vampire anymore she is a werewolf. So if that werewolf would have scratched me and not "Ly'anna" would you kill me? You are my daughter. That doesn't answer my question would you kill me as well if it were me and not her. Yes we don't need vampire/ werewolves running around. Did you kill "Ly'anna's" parents as well? Yes they were werewolves' when they died. Why can't we be both vampire and werewolf? It's just not vampirely possible to be both. It also appears that "Ly'anna" got their werewolf DNA in her as well it would seem, and that scratch kicked everything into hyper drive. With the speeds she can move if she chooses to, we couldn't fight her if she wanted to overtake the castle. So you're afraid of her because of your ego she is still a vampire, and she wouldn't hurt me or any monster else, she would do what she had to, to protect me. Just like you are willing to do whatever it takes to protect her as well it would seem. I don't see why she has to die, why can't we use the wolves' bane to help her? "Lennzie" she is a werewolf now we can't have her kind roaming free, she could kill us all in one sword strike if she really wanted too. So you will kill her, so she won't try and take your precious castle from you. So you will kill her because of your hatred and fear of werewolves taking over our lands. These are our laws that have kept us safe for thousands of years and I'm not going to change that now. Letting her live would be a crime against Nixis our lady of the night. Don't you dare bring our goddess into this; she loves all of her children of the night all equally. You speak blasphemy. No I speak truths you don't want to hear, I can't help the fact you're just too blind to see it. I will give "Ly'anna" and you until tomorrow but then she will die and you will be banished. Is that your answer then to kill her and banish your own daughter? What did you think you could win me over with your smooth talk and everything would be okay? We have laws that will not be changed for any monster. You sound like a broken religion speaking the same lines over and over again. I am the king you will show me respect. You want respect you have to give respect. People earn my respect and give me respect because I am the king. I will not show respect to an oversized spoiled no good, fang bitten slug brain like you. Enough "Ly'anna" can die and you can watch her die, before being banished. If I didn't promise "Ly'anna" I wouldn't avenge her death I'd kill you. Big talk for a small child like yourself you couldn't win in a fight against me. I beg the differ on that. "Ly'anna" will die and I am her executioner and you will watch your lover die. How can you sleep with yourself after doing this? In the dark alone, I don't regret anything I have done. Come now it's time to kill the mutt and then banish you. "Ly'anna" she doesn't have to die, I thought you still had a heart. You thought wrong I don't have a heart. "Ly'anna" is waiting to die let's not keep her waiting. Chain "Lennzie" up and keep her eyes open she will watch this. Bring out the mutt to be killed. Len...Lennzie! Lennzie my love! Ly'anna! "Ly'anna" I love you I'm sorry you have to die because of me. No! It's not your fault my love it's their hatred that is killing me not you. We will meet again soon my love. Enough talking, it's time for you to die. Ahhhhhhh! Ly'anna! Ahhhhhhhhh! Lennzie promise me you will keep your promise. I...I promise to keep my promise to you. Ly'anna! Why does she have to die! Ahhhhhhh! Crunch! Snap! Ly'anna! No! Ly'anna I love you! Ha-Ha-Ha-Ha. That was almost too much fun. Stop laughing you good for nothing fang bit. Unchain her "Lennzie" from this day hens forth you are here by banished from this castle and the nearby lands. You will be leaving here with only the clothes on your back. Great I just had to get banished just before dawn; I will need to bury myself in the desert sand to protect myself from the day time sun. I don't like the idea of being turned into vampire bacon or being turned to ashes. The sun will be coming up soon I will need to bury myself in the sand for now. Oh poor girl...losing her lover and getting banished. Right you are she can also do great things she's also some monster. Shhhhhhhh we aren't supposed to talk about that. You're right we are not here for that right now, I believe she could use this mask and cloak in her travels, so we will just leave these here for her. I was thinking the same thing as you. But we should leave for now, but we will meet again very soon my friend. Now that the sun has set I can work on my travels a bit more. What...What is this? A mask and a cloak these weren't here before. Some monster must have left them here for me but who? Also, where did this portal come from and where does it go. More importantly should I go through it? It could be better on the other side compared to this. Well here goes nothing, time to see what's on the other side. Of all places it takes me it takes me to the woods. I guess it's not all that bad I can make that cave over there home for now. I guess this will have to do for now. Now we can jump ahead in time to when I met "Anna" 'and Jarred". I can't believe it I go out hunting and come back to find these thugs in my cave. Let's see how they like waking up with some monster in their face?

Origins of Anna aka Frankin mouse

Let's go back to the beginning. My story doesn't start with a birth like most. My story is diffcrent I was created by a mad doctor. He made me to do bad things to people. But we will get to that soon enough. I was created in the basement of a teenage boy who called himself the mad doctor. He took human parts and mouse DNA and made me. It wasn't an easy feat from what he told me. He had to wait for a really big thunder storm and that was how he gave new life, to a body that was once dead. It took three tries but "Frankin mouse" came to life that day. "It's alive!" He shouted while I was getting used to my new body and learning how to use it. That day not only did I live but I danced around the room. "The mad doctor" passed his science class. Then that's when things started to get dark, he wanted me to hurt others but I couldn't find it in my heart to hurt someone else. "Hey "Frankin mouse" go hurt that person over there. Why? They haven't done anything to hurt me. It doesn't matter if they have hurt you or not they have hurt me. How did they hurt you? They call me names and push me around. They seem nice to me. I told you to go hurt them not to try and make friends with them. Don't forget I made you so you owe me your life for making you. Also, I would find it funny to watch you hurt that person as well. "No" I can't just hurt them for no reason. Why can't you hurt them I made you, you will obey me and hurt them. They seem nice to me and they give me pickles. "Frankin mouse" 'you will obey me." you will hurt that person. No! Why!? Because. Because why? They give me pickles. So let me get this straight you like them because they give you pickles? "Pickles! I love pickles they are so yummy. "Frankin mouse"? Yes doctor. I am not a pickle! Not you silly they have pickles. I'm going and getting some pickles. Hey "Frankin mouse" how are you this lovely day? I'm doing okay. Is the mad doctor trying to get you to hurt me again? Yeah he always gets mad because I won't hurt you or anyone else. Here're the pickles I usually give you. Would you still like me even without the pickles?" Yes you are a nice person you're always so nice to me. I would like you even if you didn't have pickles. I got to go but it was talking to you again "Frankin mouse" have a great day. You to pickle man thank you for the pickles. You're welcome "Frankin mouse". Hey why didn't you hurt him? Why did you try and make friends with him? He is my friend, and he likes talking to me and its nice talking to him he's my friend. You don't have any friends I made you to hurt people not make friends with them. I am your maker I created you. So? So...So that means you need to obey whatever I tell you to do. No! I'm not going to hurt anyone. You will start hurting others like I tell you or you will be left alone in this world with no friends and no one to take care of you. That's not true I have friends. don't make me laugh who would want to be friends with a goody two shoes like you. Pickle man likes me and likes talking to me. No... No one likes you to everyone else you're just a freak a creation. Why are you so faceless? faceless what do you mean faceless? Have a face but no face at the same time, you try and show me kindness but then you're bitter to everyone around you. I'm not faceless. Just can't stand people ok? You also blame me for yourself inflicted misery. Blame you no I blame them. They hit me, and call me names, so I made you to hurt them for me. But I guess I was wrong if you're trying to make friends with them. Why would you betray your maker? I didn't betray you but I'm also not hurting anyone. You betrayed me "Frankin mouse" you betrayed me by making friends with them. Why can't I be my own monster? What do you mean your own monster? I mean Dracula, Frankenstein, and that water monster are all their own monsters. You mean the creature from the black lagoon. They were freed by someone to be their own monsters. How can I be freed to be my own monster? Why would you want to be free for? I want to be able to make my own choices free to be my own monster and make friends. I'm not a mean monster; I also don't feel like a male monster. You mean you feel like a woman or Transgender? I guess you could say a little bit of both. I'm just trying to understand you right now. Why not just let me be my own monster. What do you want me to do exactly? Help me be more me, and let me be my own monster. Fine...Fine I'll help you even though you won't help me hurt people. "Thank you." I'm not doing this for you; I'm doing it for me myself not you. I don't get why you are so mean to me. I'm always kind to you. Yes that's your problem you're too nice to everyone. Why is it so bad to make friends with people? It is bad when you're making friends with the people who hurt me. They seem nice to me they have been nothing but kind to me. Compared to me they think you're a freak. Can you help me or not? I'm the only one that can help you. "Frankin mouse" I will help you with this new you thing. Please call me "Anna". Ok "Frankin"...I mean "Anna". "Anna" let's start with your name for now and go from there. After you help me are you going to keep me? I have no use for a goody two shoes like you; no after I help you I will leave you to be your own monster. Maybe I'll find other monsters like me out there in this big world. Making friends with other monsters would be nice it would be better than being alone. Okay I get it you want to meet other monsters like yourself. Now lay down on the table, so we can get started with this. Don't hate me doctor. Hate you...I can't bloody stand you, you'll be gone tomorrow. Okay let's get this over with. I'll leave in the morning if that's okay. Morning I want you gone tonight. Oh...Okay I'll be gone tonight then. Good now we can get started here goes nothing, snip, pull, tuck, fold, and done. Now get out! Okay I'm going now take care. Yeah...Yeah now get out! I'm going. I'm all alone now, nowhere to go for the night I will sleep in the woods for the night. Tomorrow I start my new life as a free monster, but for now I will get some sleep. So sad abandoned by her maker because she was too nice. That is very true, but she will do great things in time. Yes she will, but we can't talk about that right now, so we will leave this portal behind us, so she can start her new life. She will use it. For she won't be alone for very long if she does. We should get going now. This isn't goodbye my friend we will meet again soon. Its morning already the night went by pretty fast. Where did this portal come from? Better yet where does it go? I guess there's only one way to find out. It takes me into the dark woods. Now I walk through the woods, now I search for my happy ending.

Journey through purgatory

Oh man my head hurts. Hey "Jarred" are you okay? Yeah I'm fine. How about you "Azzed"? I'm alright I'm just trying to figure out where we are. Speaking of does any monster know where "Anna" is? No but I'm sure she is okay wherever she is. "Jarred" have you seen her fight? Yeah I've seen her fight remind me not to ever make her mad. Yea you can say that again I've spared with her a few times I know what you mean. Yeah well-spoken "Lennzie" but I feel bad for the poor fool who does. Agreed but I think we should also try and find out where we are before it gets dark and hard for us to see. Whooo. What's that? It looks like a Wisp? Whooo...Whooo. I think it wants us to follow it. Whoo... Whoo. Let's follow it and see where it leads us come on guys this way. Wait "Lennzie" we don't even know where it's trying to take us. I don't care "Jarred" it beats sitting here sitting on our thumbs trying to think of what our next move should be. Fair enough you make a good point, and we could use a guide out here wherever we are. Well I'm going with or without you guys. Are you sure about this

"Lennzie"? Yes "Jarred" I am. Fine then let's get going I hope you're right about this "Lennzie". Whoo...Whoo. I'm following you wisp. Whooo...Whoooo. Ok lead the way. Mind if I call you "Heylynd"? Whooo...Whooo. "Heylynd" it is. I see we are going to be traveling through the woods okay that's cool; not as cool as a forest I saw once. Hey any monster else hear that? Hear the waterfalls? Yeah we hear it, but I also hear something else to. "Lennzie" "Lennzie" come find me....I know you're here come join me we have much to talk about. I know I'm coming to find you soon. Ha-Ha-Oh really? How about we turn this into a game shall we? That's fine werewolf and prey sound good? Yes I love that game. I know you love that game. Oh and Lennzie head you're it. Hey guys we should make camp here for the night by the waterfall. Okay sounds good but who were you talking to. That was "Ly'anna" my girlfriend I am going to find her then me and her are going have a long talk about things. Okay "Lennzie" do what you need to do, and we will set up camp here. Just do us all a favor be safe and don't get lost. Yeah I can do that for you guys see you when I get back. Be safe "Lennzie", and we will see you when you get back. See you guys when I get back. Okay "Ly'anna" now it's time to find you. Ha-Ha that's if I don't find you first Ha-Ha. Wait? What? Did you just change the roles on me? Maybe I guess you will have to just find out when I find you. Not unless I find you first. You are now the prey and I am the mighty hunter I am the werewolf. Yea well I'm getting closer to you. Really? The prey sneak up on the hunter? I'm closer than you think I am. Really? Ooof yeah I'd say that's close mah I missed you so much, but we have much to talk about. I see you have met "Heylynd" He's a wisp he's been helping me on my travels through this place. But we should talk. Yes we should but where should we start? We can start with how and why you're here for starters. This wasn't by my doing if that's what you're trying to ask. Then why are you here then? My father killed me during the full blood moon. As to why I'm here I've heard that my soul can bring back a loved one who was wrongfully taken. If that is true then the stories are true then. Stories? What stories are you talking about? I also was gifted these by a riddle speaking friend of mine. I wouldn't go showing those off if I were you. You know what these are then? Yes and for you to have so many means your friends, you, and I can all get out if we can find a way out of here. So as long as we can find a way out we can use the stones to get out of here. Yes but the way out isn't a walk in the park though and will take us a few days to reach but if we work as a team we will be able to get out. There will be many dangers on our journey through this place. Speaking of this place where are we any ways? This is purgatory neither our beloved night lands, nor the realms of shadows. No we are in the place in between which is purgatory a place where souls go when they cannot enter the realms beyond. But if the stories are true then we are here for a reason as your soul and these can bring back what was wrongfully taken. But our path isn't a straight shot to the way out. No you're right it won't be a straight shot to the way out, but we can handle anything that comes our way as long as we work together as a team. "Lennzie" dangers lurk all around this place. Hey "Ly'anna" do you feel something watching us? Not to hurt us but to keep a watchful eye and make sure we are safe. We should probably get back to your friends before night fall. What happens at night fall? That's when things get very dangerous we should get back to your friends as soon as possible. Where did "Heylynd" go off to? He's probably helping a lost soul find its way or making sure your friends are safe. We should be able to get back to your friends before night fall if we follow this path we should be to your camp. We might want to stop talking for now, or we might not ever make it back to camp. Let's get going for now. Lead the way "Ly'anna" I'll follow you. Okay we should be coming up on your camp and it looks like your friends started a campfire. Yeah it looks like they did but something doesn't seem right. You're right "Lennzie" something doesn't seem right. Let's stop here and use our vampire eyes and ears to see and hear what is going on. Search the camp whoever made this fire shouldn't be too far find them. Find the fresh meat. Well "Lennzie" good news is your friends are still alive. Yeah bad news is their dead if we don't find them before those creeps do. Don't worry "Lennzie" they could be in the spot behind the falls. Whooo....Whooo. Look "Heylynd" is trying to tell us something. Whooo...Whooo. I think he's trying to tell us where your friends are. Whooo...Whooo. Let's follow him he can also help us slip by those guys, so we can see if your friends are behind the falls. What do we do if they aren't behind the falls? Maybe start hoping they are safe and Nixis is watching over them until we find them. Whooo...Whooo. Let's follow him and look behind the falls and see if your friends are there. What are we going to do if they're not behind the falls? We are going to start hoping they are safe until we find them again. Nixis will watch over them and us all you have to do is ask her. How do you know she will watch over us all? Oh just a feeling I have. You're going based on a feeling you have? "Lennzie" why not you've gone after a feeling for less. I...I... Yeah I know but this is me we are talking about I do things most monsters wouldn't even think of trying. I go after things and feelings more than most monsters would even dare to. Yeah that's true you have been known to do that many times too. I just hope this feeling of yours doesn't get us killed. We will be fine just have a little faith and all things will work out. So you think I'm going to get us killed is that it; is that what you're trying to say? No I didn't say that. Good cause if we keep fighting we will be dead ourselves if we aren't careful. Sounds like a plan. Yeah I'd say trying to stay alive is a big plan you silly Lennzie head. We should find something to defend ourselves if they find us. What about these staffs here they would make a good defense weapon if we needed to fight our way out. Hey "Ly'anna" who are these guys that are hunting my friends. "Lennzie" they are a group of cut-throats they call themselves the blood hounds. Why are they hunting me and my friends? They aren't looking for you or your friends "Lennzie" they are looking for me. You and your friends just happened to fall in the middle of everything. What do you mean "Ly'anna" what did you do? I may have killed their leader, but in my defense he tried to kill me first. Yeah well I don't think those bug brains got your memo. No they got the memo they are looking to settle the score by killing me. Yeah well these bug brains don't know who they are messing with. They aren't afraid of anything I've seen them take down a tree troll not too long ago. Yeah but they are no match for us we have taken on werewolves and won. There are also werewolves in the shadows as well and other monsters out there as well. We should find my friends before its too late. Whooo... Whooo. I think "Heylynd" is trying to tell us something. Whooo... Whooo. What is it "Heylynd" what's up? What is he saying? He says your friends aren't far from here. Whooo...Whooo. Yes right I will. What you will what "Ly'anna" what are you talking about? "Heylynd" was reminding me of something we need to talk about at some point. I see one of our me and you talks. Yes you could say that we should save that talk for another time. Your friends are close I can see them not far from us. Hey "Jarred" guess whose back. "Lennzie" Boy we are glad to see you. This beautiful angel most be "Ly'anna" it is nice to meet you. Yes "Jarred" "Azzed" this is my girlfriend "Ly'anna". It's nice to meet you "Lennzie" has talked about you a few times nothing bad she just missed you a lot. I'm "Azzed" 'and this is "Jarred" nice to meet you. Likewise to you both as well "Jarred" and you "Azzed". You are also very beautiful if I may say. Why thank you very much "Jarred" you are too kind. We should probably get some rest we have a long day ahead of us. As long as we don't run into trouble we should be able to find a way to get back to the world of the living. Yes but how do we get back even if we find, away out how are we going to go through the gate or portal to get back. I found a portal that could be our way out of here. It seems like you might need a key or something in order to get the portal to open. So we need a key or something to get through the portal. Or something. What does that mean "Lennzie"? Huh? Oh...Nothing I'll tell you when the time is right. Right now it is not the right time but hey let's get some shut-eye we have a long day ahead of us tomorrow. Goodnight every monster. Goodnight "Lennzie". Well it seems like our friends have fared well so far. Yes you are right but their path is going to only get harder the farther they travel through this realm. Yes there are many dangers everywhere in this place and many dangers they must face in the days to come. Do you think they will make it back? I think they will surprise us both, just look at "Lennzie" for instance. Yes you do make a good point there, even with everything we foresaw we still can't foresee what other out comes they will make on their own. Very true, and they are a very interesting group of monsters, even we can't fully say what is to come well we could, but they might have a different outcome then what we have seen. But we should get going, but we will be back again soon. Now we are off we will see our friends again very soon. Good morning every monster hope every monster slept well last night. Yea "me 'and "Lennzie" slept good last night. I slept alright last night. How did you sleep last night "Jarred"? I slept well last night I'm interested to see what the day has in store for us today. I think we all are but only time can truly say for sure. That is true and it's going to keep its surprises. That is true or at least not telling us. Ha-Ha that is so "Ly'anna" that is so true. You said you know of a way out? How do we get to it? It's about a four days trip from here but it's not as easy as it sounds. "It's not as simple as going from point A to point B" but we will have to take many twists and turns on our travels before we reach our journeys end. There are also many dangers that lay before us before we reach the portal and there are many paths for us to take. Let's hope we can get through the portal when we find it. Well let's get going if it's going to take some time for us to find it we are going to want to try and get to the portal as quickly as we can. Yes "Jarred" is right we should get heading out we have much ground to cover. We are going to be taking this path just ahead, and then we will follow that path until we come across a fork in the road. I take it then we can take a quick break and rest for a bit? When we get there we can rest for a little bit if we need to, however we still have a ways to go before we get there. I know I just wanted to ask. Its fine I don't blame you there I would have asked the same thing. We should be getting close to the fork in the road soon. That's good my feet are killing me. Poor "Lennzie" did you forget your hiking boots. Ha-Ha Very funny bird beak. Well I see your sense of humor is still the same as I remember. Would you love me if my humor was anything but what it is? Probably not but no matter how wild and crazy it can be at times I still love it. Yeah because my humor is as wild and crazy as I am. That is very true I've known you long enough to know that. Yes you have you've known me since we were kids. I may not have known "Lennzie" that long, but I can say I like her humor, and her bravery in combat. Yeah she does have a lot of bravery in combat doesn't she? Speaking of fights looks like we might be coming up on a fight. Good we could use a good battle. These aren't mindless thugs 'Lennzie" those are amber wood werewolves, and also not very easy to kill either. So if we do have to fight them be careful they can also be very tricky killers. Why not try and avoid them and have "Heylynd" make us invisible and sneak past them. That would work if they wouldn't be able to smell us as we tried to slip by them. Even if "Azzed" shape-shifted into one of them we still couldn't get by them. It also would help if they didn't know we were here. May I also remind you all that we don't have anything to defend ourselves with besides rocks and sticks? What are you trying to say; are we supposed to stone and stick them to death? Yeah I don't see that working out very well. Our options are fight and probably die or run for our lives and hope we get past them. I've fought and killed them before, but they are a pain in the butt to kill. Yeah let's run we can't fight them with what we have to work with. If we do need to fight aim for their heart if you can it will kill them. But now we run. Run! It looks like they are giving up the chase. I wouldn't be so sure we just got the attention of the alpha Danimo, and he is as angry as he is hungry. How do we kill it if we have to? We don't we run. We run quickly if you don't want to die a painful death run and don't look back. How will we know when we can stop running, or we have out ran the alpha Danimo. You won't hear them chasing you and they will howl to sign they are calling off the chase. They haven't done either so we keep running until then or we die whichever one comes first. We are going to turn here and head across the bridge over there. Then what do we do? We burn the bridge so it can't get across. They can't chase us if they can't get to us. That's a great idea "Lennzie" we just need to get across the bridge first without getting hit by fire arrows as well. "Ly'anna" you and the others get across the bridge I'll stay behind a bit to take out the bridge. How are you going to do that? With these. Is that? Fire bombs yes. How did you get those? No time you and the others get across the bridge I'll be right behind you guys. I'm going to burn the bridge from the middle, so they can't get across. I will be fine I will be right behind you; you will all make it across safely. What about you "Lennzie" aren't you going to make it off the bridge safely? Yes I will make it off safely as well after I stop flea boy from chasing us any farther. Do not fight me on this "Ly'anna" I know what I am doing. I hope you do just make it across in one piece. Arro! Okay wolfy it's just us now, and now you can meet fire. Taste flames flea boy. Now the flames going I am out of here bye-bye flea boy. Run! "Lennzie" run! I'm running I'm running don't get your feathers in a bunch I'm fine. Yeah well the bridge is about to snap. Yeah well I'll be safe in a second. Yeah well the bridge is breaking. Yes I can see that I am running as it's breaking you know. There I'm safe. So far it looks like "Lennzie's" plan actually worked. What are you trying to say that my plans don't work? No! I didn't say that. We should get going before it finds a way across. I agree we should make haste; we should be getting close to the fork in the road soon. Well hopefully we don't come across anymore surprises. We are coming up on the fork in the road now. Good we could use a rest and my feet are really killing me right now I could use a break. We should rest here, but we should make camp elsewhere. Yes that would probably be best if we found a safe place to rest for the night. We will be taking the path on the left. It will lead us to a safe place where we can rest for the night. We can make shelter in that cave not far from here. We should probably find that cave soon night fall is coming and the last thing we need is to be caught after night fall out here. What would happen if we did get caught in the open after night fall? We would get killed or eaten or both. Yeah good point that cave you told us about would be our safest place to rest for the night. We shouldn't be far from it now I think I see it right over there. We should check it out real quick and make sure it's empty before making camp for the night. Right we don't need any more surprises that's for sure. "Jarred" 'you and "Azzed" check the back of the cave "me, and "Ly'anna" will check out the front half of the cave. Right we don't need any more surprises like last time that's for sure. That's true "Jarred" you and "Azzed" go check out the back of the cave. "Ly'anna" and I" will check out the front of the cave. Sounds good to me "Azzed" 'you and me" go in first" then "Lennzie" and "Ly'anna" can go in next. Sure you lead the way oh fearless leader. Right I'll go check over there "Azzed" you go check over there on the other side, and we will meet in the middle. If we find anything we will let the others know what we find. Yes sounds like a plan. Hey "Azzed" it looks clear over here. Likewise, it's clear on this side too. Hey I just wanted to say I'm sorry we're dead and I wasn't able to do anything to help us. It's all good we were blind-sided by those vampires anyways there wasn't much we could've done. You are worried about "Anna" as well, aren't you"? Yeah I guess I am. Don't be she can fight if she has to, before the lights went out I saw her take on those vampires without even needing to rise a finger. I never saw her do anything like what I saw her do before we ended up here. I agree with you I didn't see what "Anna" can do but if she was dead she would have ended up here somewhere, but we need to have faith that she is alive and well wherever she is. I just hope she's not alone on the other side I don't think she is going to be sleeping well for a while after what happened to us. I hear you there but doesn't she also have those two phoenixes watching over her as well? Probably to tell the truth I'm not really sure if they are watching over her or just giving a guiding hand when needed. We should get back to "Lennzie" and "Ly'anna" and let them know the cave is clear. Hey "Lennzie" how do you think your friend "Anna" is doing". I think she's alive and doing okay otherwise we would have seen her here somewhere. I can also say after watching me die she won't be the same as she was before. That is true seeing is you also bared witness to my death and I've heard how that left you since that day. I remember that day and my father was the same one responsible for my death like he was for your death as well. Where are "Jarred" and "Azzed" do you think they are okay shouldn't they have been back by now. Its all clear in the back of the cave how are things in the front of the cave. Things are clear here as well we should work on making camp for the night. We should also try and find something to eat. Yes you are right "Jarred" we should find something to eat". I can make us a mushroom soup it's not much but it's something. Yeah that works it's better than nothing. Do you need any help with anything for your soup? No I have most of what I need for it right here. But a nice fire to cook on would be nice. "Me and "Azzed" can gather some fire wood, are you up for that "Azzed"? Yeah I'm game to help with getting some fire wood, also "Ly'anna" I want to thank you for cooking for us. You are very welcome and thank you, you are so sweet. "Jarred" and "Azzed" be careful out there. We will "Azzed" 'and I" will be back soon. "Lennzie" would you mind helping me get stuff ready for when the boys get back with the fire wood. Yeah I can help you with getting stuff ready for when they get back, what do you need help with. We have a stone bowl to cook the soup in we just need some water from the creek not far from here. I'll go get the water for the soup while you work on getting everything else ready. "Lennzie" please be really careful out there. I will I should be back before the boys get back. Okay I'll see you when you get back I'll get stuff ready for the soup. "Hey "Jarred"? Do you feel like some monsters following us or like watching over us"? Yeah now that you mention it I do. I think who or whatever is watching over us or following us might also be watching over "Anna" as well. I can't tell if who or what is watching over us is friend or foe. Same but if they were foe I'm sure they would have tried to kill us by now. Let's just hope they are friend we could us all the help we can get in this place. If they are watching over "Anna" as well I hope they are keeping her safe. Hold on "Anna" we are coming back to you soon I hope please be safe when we get back. I think we have more than enough fire wood. Hey "Lennzie" you're back the boys should be back soon. I hope they get back soon it's starting to get really dark out. I'm sure the boys are fine let's work on getting things ready for when they get back with the fire wood. We are back safe, and we're back baring wood for fire. Ha-Ha "Azzed" we can see that. I have everything else we need for the soup so it's time to start the fire and get it going before we can make the soup. I can start the fire for you. Thank you, "Azzed". You're welcome. Thank you both "Jarred" and "Azzed" for going and getting the fire wood for the soup. You're welcome "Ly'anna". Alright the fire is started; all we need to do is put the soup on then we just wait for the soup to be ready. While we are waiting on the soup why don't we talk about how we all met each other? Sounds like a great way to pass the time. I'll go first I first met "Lennzie" when we were kids, my mother and father were killed in a war or that's what I was told. I was raised by a poor family, we were a happy family. Yes I remember them and then those flea bitten werewolves came and killed them. Or even worse killed by my father, because they where werewolves. So that's why they died? Yes my dad told me about it before he killed you. I am so sorry, I've missed you every day since you died. It's true she has, and she also has terrible nightmares about that day. I met "Anna" and "Lennzie" in the dark woods I woke up to "Lennzie" standing over me. With her face in mine asking me who I was and why I was in her cave. Yes well you were in my cave so I was trying to figure out why you were in my cave, and how you would like it if some monster came into your space silly bird beak. As for me I met "Anna, Jarred, and Lennzie" when I saved them from a vampire attack. Yeah I remember I also almost kicked your butt because I thought you were my sister. Yeah well it's a good thing you didn't cause chances are I'd still be feeling it now. Yeah most likely but you'd be in a lot of pain. I'm just thankful you didn't kick my butt. I think the soup's done now. It smells really good. I hope it tastes as good as it smells, but meh food is food. It's going to be nice to have something to put into our stomachs; we are going to need all the strength we can get for the path ahead of us. Now let's eat. MMMM "Ly'anna" this is really good how did you learn how to make this. Thank you it's just something I made a few times it comes out differently every time I make it. Even so it came out really good we should probably get some rest, we have a long day ahead of us. Yes we should get some rest it is getting late goodnight every monster. Goodnight every monster. Well they made it to night two. Yes they have, but they still have far to go before they reach their journeys end. We should leave these here for them because without these they will stand little to no chance against what is to come. Yes you are right about that and there are many dangers lurking everywhere waiting to strike them at any time. Not to mention that Danimo is still on their tails. Yes but not for much longer if we throw it off their trail. How will we do that? We will have the Danimo chasing ghosts the longer it chases us the easier it is for our friends to find the portal and find their way out. True they have enough dangers ahead they don't need an alpha Danimo chasing them. Yes let it chase us the endless chase. Their days are going to get longer and more dangers are going to come from many places and carry friendly faces by the time they reach the end. Can they see through the mask and tell friend from foe or will they fall to the faceless foes to come. They will make it through the portal, and they will see through the mask of their foes. We can help them from time to time as long as we hide in the shadows if things get to crazy. Yes the last day before they reach the portal will be the most challenging day they will face. The battle to come will test them all even "Ly'anna" with her speed and her skills in battle. I could say the same thing for all of them on that note we should get going they will be waking up soon. Yes let's go. Good morning every monster. Morning. Hey any monster know where the swords and daggers came from? No but whoever left them for us knows our fighting styles for each of us. "Lennzie" there's two swords for you, "Ly'anna" two swords for you and then daggers for "Jarred" 'and myself". I don't really care where they came from, but they will be very handy for us in the days to come. The next few days are going to be longer as we get closer and closer to the portal. How much danger are we going to be facing in the days to come? Enough danger to keep us on the move. We will have a few days when we won't have time to rest or stop moving because things are going to get crazy and if we stop moving we will be as good as dead. Yeah I think it would be best to keep moving and keep going no matter what. Sounds like the closer we get to the portal the deadlier the dangers get, so we need to be careful about everything we do. Everything will try to keep us from getting to the portal we will need to watch each other's backs and watch out for each other if we are going to get through this. Yes I agree with "Lennzie" we need to use team work if we are going to make it out of here" but we should also work in pairs. Agreed "Azzed" 'and I" will be one team". "You 'and "Lennzie" can be the other team, but we will cover each other if needed. Agreed if we work together as a team the four of us will make a killer team. That's so true "Azzed" we would make a killer team. Thank you, "Lennzie". You're welcome anytime shifter boy. The next few days are going to test our team skills to the limits. What are some of the dangers we should look out for in the days ahead? We could be facing Ghouls, Goblins, Fairies, Demons,

Vampires, Werewolves, Huntsmen, and many more dangers. We will need team work and maybe a miracle to get out of here. Hey guys I think we should pick up those swords and daggers something is moving around out there. We should also get heading out, or we could get trapped in here if those are enemies out there. "Lennzie" here're two swords for you, "Ly'anna" here is two swords for you, and "Azzed" two daggers for you and these bad boys are mine. Right now we're off. We will be following this path over here until we can't follow it anymore then we will take another path from there. I'm sure we will also face many dangers on our path ahead. Why don't we focus on the here and now why don't we? Well looks like we got a fight closing in on us. Let them come we can take them what are we facing. Aromons. What is an Aromon? An Aromon is a mix between Angel, Demon. So they are like nightmares that move like lighting then. Well looks like this fight will really test our reflexes because here they come. RReee! They're coming get ready. Wait what? Zip. Zip. Zip. Zip. Zip. Thud. Thud. Thud. Thud. Thud. What the shadow just happened? Elves is what happened don't let their good looks and charm fool you they are very deadly hunters. Yes but from where I'm standing we also helped you with your little Aromon problem. Yes but we didn't ask for your help did we elf boy. "Lennzie" do not anger them we could use the help. Fine no fighting elves I got it. So what do you say "Athoma"? Will you help us? I will help you get to the portal any way we can help you get there. I have a member of my kin on the other side. Do you want me to give her a message for you? Yes let her know I love her dearly and I'm sorry I didn't say goodbye I hope one day she can forgive me. I can do that for you what is her name? She calls herself "Sal" because her name is hard for some monsters to say. Thank you for helping us. You are very welcome also your riddle speaking friends told us where you were, they also paid us a large amount of supplies my tribe needs in these times. What do you mean these times? You haven't noticed the dark clouds and the increase of monsters lately. Oh so that's what you are talking about. Yeah that's not the first time our riddle speaking friends have done something like this before. What do you mean "Lennzie"? Do you remember "Sondra" from that desert town? Yes why? Do you remember the lizard's teeth she had that covered everything we needed and a hundred times over? Now that I think about it yeah I remember that. Hey elf boy what did these friends say to you that was a riddle to you. They told me my kin member on the other side is safe and said she is with two others. But how would they know that. I don't know they seem to know a lot of strange things but won't say how or why they know what they do. We should keep going we have a lot of ground to cover. You also have a six-day journey as well before you reach the portal my friend. What about the portal that I found not far from here? Your friend told us that one is a fake and told us how to find the real one. The portal will open when the serpent ends. What does that mean? I think it might have to do with these snake creatures. That might be a good start but it could also be the hydra of the city of Endenhower think we can talk and move at the same time. Yes me and my men will cover you from the tree tops we will take this one path at a time shall we. I have a question how do we know the portal will open or not. I don't think we can tell we will have to wait and see. Hey elf boy what can you tell us about the city of Endinhower? It was once a great and wealthy city. It had food, shelter, and stores for anything you could ever need here, and trade markets, a very wealthy bank, fur traders and much more. But when the hydra came everything changed the town's people called it Emitor which means the bringer of death or the destroyer. Will we have to travel through Endenhower before we reach the portal? Yes we will before your journey is complete. "Athoma". Where are we heading before we get to Endinhower. Nowhere "Ly'anna" we are heading straight to Endinhower. Hey elf boy what are we facing on the road ahead. Aromons, and werewolves. "Jarred" keep your daggers ready for a fight. "Azzed" you do the same as well. So "Athoma" How long until we reach Endenhower? It's about three days away from here. Okay elf boy how will we know we are getting closer to Endenhower. "Lennzie" stop calling him that. "Ly'anna" you know it's a part of who I am. Let her be "Ly'anna" "Lennzie" is fine. Will we find places for us to rest along our path? There will be a few caves but not anything I'd advise you to seek shelter in. but we need all the rest we can get. Yes but as we get closer you can't afford to get rest for a second rest could mean either life or death. We will be taking the path on the left up ahead. This almost seems to easy there is usually Argonauts all over the place. Well I think they found us because here they come. This should be an easy battle they sound slow and dumb. Oh "Lennzie". I like you're fighting spirit". However, they are really hard to kill for their weak spot is on their back or their heart. Why not just cut them in half and call it good. "Lennzie" have you ever tried to stick a stick through a dragon's skin. No why? Because that's what it's like, trying to break through Argonauts thick armored skin. Well this should be fun. Here they come show them the sting of our blades. They're almost upon us. Yeah we can see that elf boy we have eyes. Let's team up. Grarrrr. That's right beasty come to my blade. I could end this fight a lot faster if I use my super speed. By all means "Ly'anna" go ahead and do that. Wush Thud. Well I'll be covered in honey and fed to a bear; she killed all sixteen Argonauts in seconds. I've seen vampires and werewolves speedy movements, but I've never seen a vampire/werewolf move like she moved having the speed of both Vampire/Werewolf. Okay you can stop gawking at my girlfriend anytime now. My dear "Lennzie" I wasn't gawking at "Ly'anna" I was simply admiring her speed. Good now can we get moving before it gets dark out. Yes we should be getting closer to the path ahead. Okay elf boy lead the way. Hey "Athoma" what kind of things should we look out for in Endenhower? We will be fighting Emitor and many snake demons as well and anything else that has claimed Endenhower as their home. That helps a little bit. No it doesn't I don't think even elf boy knows what we are going to face in there. I mean other than that hydra who can meet the sting of my blade. I'd have to say "Lennzie" has a good point". So elf boy is just as much in the dark as we are on what we will be facing in Endenhower. We don't know what we are going to fight in Endenhower, where is your warrior spirit now "Lennzie". I still have it don't you worry about that elf boy. You say that but I sense fear. Why don't you come down here and see just how much fear I don't have. Very tempting but we have more pressing matters at hand. Like what elf boy. Food, drink, and shelter for the night for starters. Fine I will spare you some other time. Yes you shall sometime. But "you and "Ly'anna" need to feed. Elfish blood will give you the strength you need for the battles to come. It should but "Athoma" are you sure about this". "Ly'anna" I wouldn't have said you are going to feed if I didn't want to feed you. Yes but I just wanted to ask and make sure. Hey elf boy how do you plan on feeding us? My dear "Lennzie" you and "Ly'anna" aren't the first vampires I've fed in my days. You'll be feeding from my wrists don't worry we will do it away from your friends. Fine elf boy lead the way I'm starting to get hungry. Follow me behind those trees over there. "Omanien" watch the others for a bit. Yes sir. We will be back soon take the others and find food we will be back before you know it. Yes sir. Why does she say yes sir when you talk to her? Because she is a good warrior and I am her leader. Now you can feed you need not fear hurting me I will be fine. "Athoma" thank you for letting us feed from you". Shhhhhh just feed "Ly'anna" you need your strength you will need all the strength you can get and with Elfish blood you will get all the strength you need for the anything that lays ahead of you. For where we are going you will need all the strength you can get. Do you think we will have the power to kill the hydra and get out of here alive? My dear I think you and your friends can kill Emitor and his snake demons. The battle you will face in Endenhower will test everything you know in battle and push your skills to the limit. We should be getting back to camp now and get some rest. Goodnight every monster. Goodnight

"Athoma" thank you for all you've done to help us. Do you think they are ready for the battle ahead of them? Maybe but they will also need these to help them kill the destroyer when the time is right. "Althes" is that? Yes it's a dragon blade made from the bone of an ancient dragon and a scale of a hydra dipped in the sacred stream of the hidden monks. This is the only sword that can kill Emitor, the sword requires a great level of skill and some small amount strength to use, but they can handle them with ease. If any monster can use this sword it's "Lennzie" or "Ly'anna". But we can't also forget about the daggers for "Jarred" and Azzed" they can use with great skill. Ah yes the drake blades said to be able to cut through anything like butter. To any snake demon or other creature they will look like just a boring blade. We must be going, but we will be checking in on our friends again soon. Good morning every monster. What the...Where did these come from? Who cares where they come from we could use these in our battle in Endenhower. I think I know who left them for us and why they left them for us. "Jarred" Azzed" here's a set of daggers for you two. There's also a sword for you "Ly'anna" and one for me". Well whoever left them knew you would need them they can kill most things, but they can't kill the hydra. If whoever left these for us knew we needed them; they may also know when to give us what we need when the time is right. Whoever left these knows each of our fighting styles and maybe even more. Whoever they were gave you what you needed at the right time. There will be more battles the closer we get to Endenhower. You will also be getting less and less sleep. So hopefully you got as much sleep as you could because from here on in you won't be getting much sleep. Is that why you also did what you did for "Ly'anna" and me last night. We have a three days journey ahead of us; we will be taking the path on the left. Hey "Lennzie" how do you think "Anna" is doing? I'm sure she is doing good "Azzed", I believe she is doing okay". Us being gone has probably been really hard on her. Same and she will love "Ly'anna" just as much as she loves "Lennzie". Aww Lennzie head from what I've heard you say about her she seems kind and sweet I like her already. That's nice you four but you should really focus for now enemies could rain down on you at any time. We all need to be on guard enemies can pop up anywhere. We need to stay alert enemies lurk above and below your heads and feet. Yes we get it elf boy this isn't the first time we have seen battle. Yes but have you faced snake demons before? No but my sword says let them taste the sting of my blade. I don't know if you're crazy, reckless, or just battle hungry. I'm a mix of them all I guess but I've won most my battles. But you lost a battle or you wouldn't have ended up here. Whether I lost a battle or not I would have ended up here eventually anyways. You listen to me elf boy I'm here for a reason. Looks like you can test your blades Argonauts are heading your way. "Azzed" and "Jarred" you take the left half "Ly'anna" and me' will take the right half". Let's make them go running back home to mommy. Lennzie head you always make me laugh with your sense of humor in the mist of battle. Yeah that's our "Lennzie" for you always making jokes in the face of danger. Come feel the sting of my blade I'll send you crying home to your mommy come on beasties. Grarrrr. Taste my blade Swish... Shink. Thud. Well dip me in honey and call me a flower these swords and daggers cut through them like butter. Hey "Lennzie" friendly challenge to see who can kill more? You're so on get ready get set kill. Swish... Shink... Thud. 5. 10. Dang they are easy to kill I'm already at 20 kills. 20? I have 15 kills. They're running away to mommy. I got 10 kills. What about you "Azzed"? I got 10 kills too "Jarred". "You and "Azzed" are tied and "Lennzie" came in second and I came in first place this battle. Well I'll be a fish's uncle you four took on 50 or more Argonauts and won. Yeah we did elf boy you seem surprised like you didn't think we could do it. Maybe you can with those swords and daggers you also seem to be getting stronger and faster with every kill. So elf boy you mean to tell us the more kills we get in battle the stronger and faster we will become. Yes we could use that while we are fighting that hydra.

You will fail no matter how strong or fast you get you will not win in there. One question still remains where did they come from? I think I know who left them for us. Who do you think it was "Lennzie"? The same ones who left the lizards teeth we needed. Anytime we need something it seems to show up around the time we need it. If that's the case maybe we will have something to kill that Emitor with when the time is right. Maybe we will have to see how things go. Hey elf boy how close are we to Endenhower? We still have a day or two travel left until we get there. Anything we should look out for as we get closer to days Endenhower. Dangers will be all around you from above and below you and anywhere in between. We can handle anything that comes our way elf boy danger can come and taste the sting of my blade. "Lennzie", you are so egger to face danger". To hide how scared you really are that you make jokes so no one sees how scared you really are. Why don't you come down here and find out just how little scared I really am. Big words for some monster that is so small. Who are you calling small elf boy you talk a big game for some monster who attacks enemies from a tree. "Lennzie" what are you doing". Elf boy told us danger lurks above us and below us and also said it will test us to see if we can tell friend from foe. What do you mean? What I mean is I think elf boy and his men have been kidnapped and replaced with clones. The real elf boy would have tried to help us even if he knew his arrows wouldn't kill those Argonauts we faced the other day. He wouldn't have sat and watched us be attacked by monsters out numbering us 50 or more to 4 he's not the real elf boy. Well seems like she is too smart for her own good but no matter you and your friends are not making it out of here alive. You can't save your friends. Yeah well we will see about that won't we elf boy wanna be. I guess we will soon but not here we will see you soon little ones when we meet again you will die. Where did they go? I think they went back to Endenhower I don't think we will be getting much rest for the next few days we shouldn't be far from Endenhower now before elf boy was kidnapped by that wanna elf boy be he told us we were about a day away from Endenhower. Yes but we shouldn't waste too much energy on things right now. Sorry we didn't trust your intuition "Lennzie". Its fine, just listen to me when I tell you something doesn't seem right. Deal we can do that. We should keep moving we can't afford to rest; we are getting closer to Endenhower from the looks. Well looks like we won't have wait too long to settle the score with fake elf boy. We should see if we can help them before we try and fight Emitor we are going to need all the help we can get in this fight. You're right we should search the buildings and see if we can find them. I think I know where we might find them it seems like they might be in that building over there if my ears don't fail me. Let's go check it out we should have two keep watch and look out for any danger that could come our way. "Ly'anna" you and "Jarred" will stand guard. "Azzed" and I" will go in and search for elf boy and his men. Sounds like a plan you two be safe in there. You be safe out here if you see or hear anything let us know. You do the same we will "Azzed" follow me" we will work together. Yes ma'am I got your back. Right let's get in there and see what we find. Dang it's old looking in here and dusty. Yeah it looks like this place has been left to fall to ruin as time goes by, this place looks like it has seen better days. Shhh listen I think I hear something. Like what. Is any monster out there? Help us. That sounds like elf boy. Why do you call him that? Because it's part of who I am. Why are you jealous? I didn't give you one yet? What no. Yeah you are. No I don't care about silly nicknames why should I care about something like that. Well if you say so. I think that sound is coming from over here if you want to check it out. Yea we should we might want to ready our weapons in case we need them can't be too safe in a place like this. "Lennzie" is that you? We are in here you need to find a way to get through that wall they trapped us in here and built that wall around us. Now curious how did you know to come looking for us here? Your clone tried to lead us a stray and was going to kill us but I caught on to his plan. Well thankfully you found us. We will need your help to defeat Emitor can you help us, and we can even leave your evil clones for you to take care of. Sounds like a deal to me. You will need to find something to break through the wall with but it will draw attention to us if you do are you sure about this. Yes we aren't going to leave a friend behind we will help you. But what will break through this. "Lennzie" I think we can use these to cut through the stones. It's worth a shot it might work. Here goes nothing. Clang! Well I'll be they cut through those stones like butter. Looks like your idea worked "Azzed" now elf boy we should get going and regroup with the others. Elf boy? Yes "Lennzie". We should get out of here I have a score to settle with that clone wearing my face those snake demons are going to pay for they are also shaped shifters that's why they could look like us. We will find them and you take care of Emitor we will clear out most of the snake demons. Will we see you after this battle? Maybe not but after you are done here the portal isn't far away but dangers will be everywhere trying to stop you from making it back to the living world. What brings you to Endenhower little ones? Are you looking for death? We are looking for Emitor so we can kill him. Well you have found him for he is I. where are you are hiding in the shadows like a scared little monster. Who are you to bid me insult. I am "Lennzie " you over sized snake with four heads. What makes you think you can kill me. That is for me to know and you to find out when you taste the sting of my blade. I see my demons failed at killing you. Yes they did I knew they weren't the real elf boy and his men. How did you know? I can tell my friends from my foes? You are smarter than you look but you are still foolish if you think you can kill me no matter how much help you muster to try and kill me you will fail. That's what your snake demons told us too, but you see we have one thing you can't beat. Oh and what is that little vampire. We have team work and we have each other's back. You think that will stop me or the armies of demons I have at my side. It doesn't matter how many demons you think you have we can overcome anything if we work together. We will see about that enough talk it's time to die. Get ready every monster it's time to fight this oversized worm with four heads. You four think you can kill me? I am death no monster can kill me. Yeah well we will see about that now won't we you worm. You think you're so strong because of your thick skin, but you're wrong. What's this you think you have a chance to kill me. You know for a worm you put up a big talk. Yes you are right now it's time. It's time for you to die. Right now you can taste the sting of my blade. Ready every monster this is going to be the longest fight we have had to fight. Die. Swish. Duck! Clang! I think we stand a chance now fight! Fight. Look out. Clang. We need to last as long as we can I'm sure we will get what we need to kill this worm when the time is right. but we don't know when that time will be. No we don't, but we need to believe we can do it or else we will die. Gee nice pep talk "Lennzie" that was kind a good. Thank you, bird beak. Wush. You know I don't think now is the best time to be having a talk about how to fight we need to break up into two groups. Right it will be harder for that worm to attack us if we split into two groups. "Lennzie" and I" will go left "you and "Azzed" will go right". We can do this trust me we have your back. Crash! Duck! We got this! Over here you gutless bug you think you can claim ownership over anything you want. These lands don't belong to you nor will they ever belong to you. This land is mine I stole it from these weak creatures while they ran for their lives. We are here to reclaim their home land, so they can live in peace once more. Once more? You claim to believe there was peace in these lands before me. Swish! Crash! There will always be death and I will bring it to the weak. These people are not weak. Clang! Sheek. What you think you can get through my thick skin. No but like all things even you have a weakness it's just a matter of finding out what that weakness is and where it is. I have no weakness I will break you all. You can't break us we will rise up from every blow we take. You won't leave here alive no matter what you do. There is no way you can beat me. Yeah well we will see about that in time now won't we? "Lennzie" look out oof. "Ly'anna" are you okay? Yeah I'm fine, don't worry about me. Clang. You think you can break my skin and kill me there is nothing that can kill me. Yes you said that you giant coward you think you can't be killed but anything can be killed if you think you can't die you will die. You talk a big talk for some monster who's going to die. You can try, but we will show you the might of the vampire. "Lennzie" the sun is setting and giving light to a full moon. We have this fight we just need to believe in ourselves. Crash! Clang! What are you waiting for you can't win against me. I am your death. That's what you think, but we will win this battle not you. The moon is out now "Ly'anna" let's show him the speed of the vampire and the werewolf. Yes we shall. Swish. Clang. Crash. Swish. Clang. Crash. What how are you moving so fast you are no normal vampire what are you? I am your end you spineless gutless worm you think you are going to survive this battle but you will be the one to die. Enough talk now you die! Rrrrr! "Ly'anna" Catch. Rrrr! Swish. Grah. Huh? What how? What? I can't lose to any monster. Yeah well you lost to us. This is a curious blade where did it come from? I thought you gave it to me. No the blade came from the trees. Do you think elf boy gave it to us when we were so close to getting killed? No I don't think it was him, but we don't know for sure but what does it matter we made it out of that battle. We should get going elf boy said we should keep going because we might not see him again after this battle. But if he's listening I want to thank him for helping us we would have never made it this far without his help. We are not far from the portal now we have maybe a day or two's travel before we reach our journeys end. I think that blade that killed Emitor was only a one time use to kill it and no other from the way it just kind a turned to ashes after we killed the great hydra. We can make it out of here if that's what you guys are worried about. I have a feeling things are going to get better for our friends they are so close to the portal now. Yes they are thankfully that sword from the legends worked. So we were just as thankful as they are that the sword worked then. Yes. But there are more twists for our friends and the road ahead will get harder and the greatest sacrifice will be made but our friends will all make it out of here. But we can't say who might almost get left behind. Anyways we should let them get back to our friends. Right they should there is much to come they don't want to miss out on the things to come. Hey "Lennzie" we should be close to the portal now is it just me or does it seem to be getting darker and darker as the days seem to pass as we make our way closer to the portal. Well thankfully we still have our other weapons because it looks like we are fighting our way out of here. Just keep going we can make it out of here the portal isn't that far we are closer to it than we thought I see it over there. Oh great there's also enemies all over the place how are we going to make it out of here. We will make it out of here. "Ly'anna" you make sure "you, Jarred, and Azzed" make it out I will be right behind you I can take these thugs on. No "Lennzie" I'm not going to lose you after getting you back. You are not losing me and there is no time to argue about this I'm staying to buy you time to get through the portal. Go now I will see you on the other side. How do you know you will make it back? I have faith in Nixis to watch over me and make sure I get back safe. "Ly'anna" we have to go we can't stand here we need to go. "Lennzie" make haste to meet up with us on the other side. I will. Come on come and get me you brainless worms. Who you are you calling brainless worms you little brat. We will show you who the brainless one is after we remove your brain and eat you. No thank you I won't be the one dying or getting eaten. Come on catch me if you can. Ahhh get back here you little brat. "Ly'anna" we need to get through the portal now she is making the sacrifice she wants to make, so we can make it through the portal if she says she will see us on the other side she will see us on the other side now we need to go. Where are we? This isn't where we died. No it's not but your friends are in a camp not far from here. Who are you? Where are my manners? My name is "Claire" I am a seer I see things before they happen and things to come. You are worried about your girlfriend I can safely tell you she will be here safely behind you just give her some time to catch up with you. I'll be here when she gets back. Go wait for her with your friends. They will be happy to see you have returned safely. After you have all been reunited you will all have a long journey ahead of you. Now get going and wait for your girlfriend she will be here before you know it. Okay and thank you "Claire" for telling us where we can find our friends and waiting for us to make it back safe. No problem dear it's all part of what I do now go get some rest you need it after what you went through there in purgatory. Yes we are off to go get some rest. What where am I? How did I get back?